Women Of Forgotten Importance

Lexi Wolfe

LEXI WOLFE

Copyright © 2018 Lexi Wolfe

Front Cover Photograph © Andrew Slade

Back Cover Photograph © Dennis Wright

Author Photograph © Matt McLennan

Cover Design: Andrew Slade

All rights reserved.

ISBN: 9781980289111

DEDICATION

This book is dedicated to my fellow women, both past and present, whose songs have gone unsung and stories gone untold for the past few thousand years.

You are strong.
You are capable.
You are enough.
Keep going.

LEXI WOLFE

CONTENTS

ACKNOWLEDGEMENTS	7
INTRODUCTION	9
The Witch In The Woods	11
Introduction	11
The Witch In The Woods	13
Mrs. Oscar Wilde	33
Introduction	33
Mrs. Oscar Wilde	36
The Pendle Witch	64
Introduction	64
The Pendle Witch	67
Final Note By The Author	109
Select Bibliography	111
ABOUT THE AUTHOR	114

LEXI WOLFE

ACKNOWLEDGEMENTS

This book might never have been collated, and the words herein never written, were it not for those who have been my enablers - those who have given their support, time and occasionally their money towards my acting and writing crafts over the years. Acting, and producing your own work, takes dedication, time, energy, focus, research, having to make scary phone calls, your own money, and a portion of your sanity. And yet it is one of the most spiritually rewarding jobs I have personally encountered, not least when someone appreciates your work. Thank you to all the people who have helped me along this part of my journey:

Firstly and foremost, my best friend, my manager, my flatmate and my most encouraging critic - Andrew Slade, whose expertise, friendship and belief in me has essentially meant I have been able to continue and grow, doing what I love. My life would look very different were you not in it.

My mother, Avril, for also being continually giving of her time and support, arranging coaches for her and her friends to come and see my shows when they were in town (and when they were not), and for giving me notes after every show of mine she's ever attended(!)

To my father, Timothy, without whom I never would have gotten through LIPA.

Paul Good & Rachel Lawson, my southern parents, another pair without whom I would have been in dire straits these past couple of years. You have gone above and beyond so many times, and I am so grateful.

Keely Saunders, for her friendship and use of her lovely house (and flat by proxy), and for coming to every show she can.

Andy Naughton, my first techie, who pushed me to do more, then made it necessary I do so. I know it wasn't intentional, but my dreams started to come true after what you taught me. I'm very grateful.

Jean, his mother, for showing me why women like Constance Lloyd's stories are in desperate need of telling, and what happens when they are forgotten.

And, of course, an incredibly grateful bow in the direction of all those who have followed, supported, bought tickets, spread the word, ooh'ed and aah'ed, left reviews, put up pictures and generally been great sources of comfort and happiness to me while I perform my shows.

Thank you all. I couldn't do this without you!

INTRODUCTION

Something I noticed as a young woman was that if one looks at history, one sees a startling imbalance. One could drown in the number of stories of men that pepper the textbooks, but there seem so few, in comparison, of women.

Initially, of course, I fell for the rhetoric that because we were predominantly child-bearers, child-rearers and physically somewhat feebler than men, we had therefore somewhat involuntarily taken a backseat throughout the Timeline from the beginning of recorded history to this moment, in favour of our more heroic male counterparts.

But then one comes across characters like Boudicca. Joan of Arc. Elizabeth I. Emmeline Pankhurst and Emily Wilding Davison. Sacagawea. Rosa Parks. Mary Wollstonecraft. These women didn't conform to the Helen of Troy damsel-in-distress figures I'd come to expect, wherein the female haplessly and stereotypically awaits for male rescue. These were angry, feisty, kickass women who didn't care what gender they had been born into - they had stuff to get done, things to change, people to save and liberate, and they were going to get it all done in spite of, and because, they were women.

From there, it is only a hop, skip and a jump to realising that women have always been there, ready and active at recorded historical events, but because our positions have not always been those of power, one might easily assume - our own daughters might assume - that women have not been active participants in the changing of laws, the throwing off the shackles of oppression or the events which so keenly define our cultures and society even today. It might be mistaken that we have continuously been nothing but the arm candy for the history-makers. And on occasion, that summation is true. However, is it not possible that that is simply how we have mostly been conditioned to behave, and that those who rebel against this are seen as the exception?

The Romans told Boudicca and her daughters, in the most violent of terms, that they were not entitled to the land belonging to Boudicca's late husband, and to be grateful for the charity their overlords had left them. Boudicca did not accept that answer. She rallied her people, gathered an army and razed three of the largest cities the Romans built to the ground, one after the other.

Joan of Arc was probably barely even noticed before she received a sign from God to take back France from England - a young female with no military training, and yet she too led armies, reinstated the birthright of a king and eventually became a saint. This younger Boudicca was also subject to the most unimaginable cruelty when she was consigned to the flames, and yet there is something deliciously terrifying in the idea that a young woman can accomplish so much in, not only a male-dominated society, but one which had not even yet formally identified women as their own entities beyond their male connections.

History, however, has long been cruel to females. Not only can it embellish men's tales, but it often does not acknowledge when we have either accomplished something, or have had great wrongs done to us. These are stories which, in my humble opinion, are also valid and are in danger of being forgotten. To take only the example of invention - What of the likes of Ada Lovelace, overlooked as the world's first computer programmer? Instead she is remembered chiefly as Lord Byron's daughter. Or Lise Meitner, German-Jewish refugee of the Nazis, co-inventor of Nuclear Fission, unmentioned by her partner Otto Hahn in 'his' works? Or even Hedy Lamarr, whose work gave birth to many wireless inventions we would be lost without today, whose involvement is only now somewhat more common knowledge?

The following are stories about women throughout history who have not held swords aloft, but who have suffered. With the little that is gathered about women such as these, there is only so much fact one can make sure is in place, and have the rest be supposition. But these three women, for reasons even to this day I can't quite fathom, spoke to me from their positions of despair, sorrow, determination, defiance and made sure I knew that their tales were worth telling.

While out of chronological order in terms of a timeline, these stories are presented here in the order in which I wrote them, originally for the stage.

ID# The Witch In The Woods

Introduction

The Witch In The Woods was my first one woman show, inspired by a production I saw in Edinburgh at the Fringe Festival in 2014. Two young women presented an adaptation of the story of 'Harry The King' (Shakespeare's *Henry V*) with just the two of them as cast - Lucy Fyffe was Harry, and Sally O'Leary was everyone else. Their props were minimal, as was their set: a large white sheet was used as a backdrop, turned over to see blood on the other during the battle scenes, and used to emulate the sea. Precious little else was used or, indeed, needed. The whole story was brought down to just under an hour. I spent the entire time wide-eyed and completely in belief of the story I was being presented. That one performance inspired something in me that chased me for days following:

"If they can do so much, and make me feel so deeply, with so little… Then what can I do?"

With only a vague idea of subject matter, but more determination than I'd felt in a long while, I booked myself a slot at the Lewisham Fringe Festival, less than three months away. *The Witch In The Woods* was written by the beginning of October.

It was a story I felt had not really been told to a modern audience: it is a historical story about a cunning woman, the kind of person who would later be called a 'witch'. When the play opens, she has in recent times taken up living in a shack in the woods, due to being ostracised by the spread of Christianity, and its new power over her village.

A woman exactly like Maya, as I called her, could well have existed, and her circumstances and the things which happened to her are far from inconceivable. That was part of my design. I wanted my audience to realise what happens to the people who are ostracised. How they are demonised for their differences, and how a simple, slow and subtle change of public opinion can be their undoing; that their whole lives can be irrevocably affected, that their very lives can be in jeopardy because public opinion is not with them. This story may sadly be relevant for many years, if the U.K. and other western nations continue to treat their immigrants, refugees, second and third generation citizens, the poor, the disabled and the elderly, in the shocking way that they seem compelled to do at the time of my writing.

The Witch In The Woods had its debut at the London Theatre in New Cross Gate, London, in November 2014, both my first written one woman show, and the first one woman show I had ever written to be performed.

Oh, if only I could scare myself witless each time I step onstage now!

LEXI WOLFE

The Witch In The Woods

Who goes? Who goes at my door? Who comes?

Strangers! Strangers come to my door. I don't know your faces, and I know each I've met before, from knee high to this height, I remember.

So, you can't be from the village, or else I'd know you. You wouldn't be from there anyway, not coming to my door and yet looking so brazen and fearless. Travelling, is it, that brings you to my door? Even though it be winter time? ...You've heard there's more food in the south. I often hear the same in winter. Run out of your stores already, have you? Not the best harvest this year? And a cold winter like this makes one eat all the more just to stay warm. So you travel looking for more food.

I never thought that travellers to the south would stop at my door before the village... And, you see, I've only so much space here. Perhaps it would be far better if only you stayed in the village instead. There'll be more space for all there, and some food, of course, in exchange for coin. And why, it is not so hard to come by! To get there, carry on along the road by which you came, keep the stream to your right, and the village can't be missed...

Well, be off then! It may be cold, but you'll not catch your death for that short a walk.

...But far be it from me to throw strangers from my door on a cold winter night such as this. Very well! You can stay. You'll have to make use of what space you can find. Just! - don't eat everything that you see and don't touch what you don't know what it may be! I'm not a woman to be crossed. I'll see what I can fetch together for us to eat. But! If you're staying another night, you'll have to find another something yourselves. It's hard enough feeding myself just now, never mind guests as well. Aye, well. Be at home in my home for the time that you are here. I'll see what I can make for us to have for some kind of supper....

Can't even think when the last time I had visitors must have been! No, I do. Must have been springtime. They too were travelling south, but for different reasons. Dane men had come to their land. Their village was put to the sword, and those that lived came this way. No! It must have been summer. I remember now - we found blackberries and elderberries, so must have been the end of summer.

You're lucky you came this way, though. I don't know how many you get at home, but that wood out there you came through? Why, it's crawling with wolves.

Did you not hear them as you came this way? They don't bother me much, as I've a better mind than to bother them, but... I hear them more than I see them. And when I hear them, I shut my door and don't go forth until I hear them again. They howl as the hunt begins, you see, and then they howl once more to round themselves up and go home when the hunt is done. All kinds of wolves. Ones that you see from a distance and think might be tame enough, little enough. Others, you wouldn't dare go near, nor let them see you. Hundreds of wolves out there in those woods, for all I know. When you can't count how many different howls you hear, you're best off staying behind doors. It's said they don't like the taste of man's flesh, but I'm happier for having my door than I am for finding out!

You must think I'm simple, mustn't you? 'This poor, simple woman!' Living out here by myself, wolves at my door. Any offensive men that may come by. Away from everyone else. And what happens if I get sick?

Ah - I don't get sick. Others get sick; and then, they come here. They come to find me.

It's better I live out here anyway. They talk a lot of nonsense about me back in the village, so if you do go onto them in the morn, don't listen too hard to it. I've heard all their stories. They said the same of my mother, too - worse. They called her a hag, said that she was an evil woman. They said that if you came near our house, she'd drown you in the stream, or that if you were a little child and you came to us alone, she'd eat you to stave off her hunger. None of it true. My mother was rather fond of children – and no, NOT to eat.

But that's reason enough for me to live here instead of the village. I like it better here anyway. Everything I need. Don't get disturbed very often. I've my own crop yard outside for the warmer seasons and the stream, as you saw, runs close by my house. What more could I want?

What was that? No, no... There's no man. Not for me, never was. What would I want for, anyway? What are they any good for? I do well enough without a man getting in my way. Spoiling my work. Making problems for me.

Are you weary, travellers, then? Might you be somewhat restored with a tale? I know a tale of a man who caused problems for his wife, and you now remind me of it.

Many years ago, when we lived back in the village, my mother had a woman come to her for help, because of her husband. I was at my mother's knee, but I remember very well. She came into our home with tears in her eyes, this woman, her face all puffy and red.

"Elvina. I have tried to stay away. I've tried the longest time, but now I cannot. It's my man, Elvina! He's mine and he has been for years, but I know that he lies with others when he does not lie with me....Have you heard of it?...How many know? Am I the only one who has believed him when he says he honours me? Has he lain with you?...But he tried to, didn't he?

"My neighbour's husband had been near two years dead when she starts to grow fat with child. 'How lucky for you!' we say. 'Where comes this miracle baby from?' we laugh. But I could not laugh today, Elvina. Her young boy is now just walking. As he played out in the way near my door this morning. I looked down and into the child's face… And a face so like my husband's, that I dared not breathe, did stare back at me!

"When my husband returned tonight, he laughed when I spoke to him on it. But I would not let it rest, as he wanted. I asked, and asked, until he stopped laughing, and asked again. Then he beat me as you see, told me to be quiet. Taunted me for how I should not be surprised he lies with other, when I give him nothing but daughters, that perhaps he will go and take up with another, then see how I fare and see that I should hold my tongue…

"I don't have much, but… I'll give you whatever I can. He's mine, Elvina. No others. He's mine, and mine alone."

My mother listened to this woman's sorrows, and soothed her. She sat her down, looked among her things, and gave this woman sow's thistle. She told her to put it in everything that her husband ate or drank and not let it be seen. And this woman, as so many had done before, she trusted my mother's words, and in it went. She used it in his morning's draught, to cover his bread, to make his bowl of stew – in it went day after day.

Some nights after first she starts this, this woman's husband takes himself up with a maid: a pretty young thing that was easily flattered by his words. Out they are a-walking when he complains he does not feel too well. She, being a kindly girl, takes him to her father's house close by to give him some broth, but still he charms throughout his discomfort, and they talk and she feels a sadness for his discomfort. It almost came to a moment of tenderness between them.... When, without warning or the husband being able to stop, a great rumble from below is heard and with a sudden tremendous stench and a weakness to his legs, the husband suddenly loses himself, and soils himself all over her father's house.

Well this is most unexpected, especially from the young maid who stands so near to him. She, with great horror, screams and swiftly, for so they will come to hear their daughters shriek as she did then, in comes the father! He sees all in a moment - a married man lying on his floor, wall to wall with filth, alone with his young daughter, who's a-quivering and a-shaking! And this father, he picks the dirty fellow up and throws him from his house, racking him a good going with his stick 'til he reaches his own door!

The husband not so admired by the young maids when that story was told, I tell you! And told it was! For years, all one had to do was say the husband's name and everyone about the village might begin to laugh, or you'd know someone meant to say that they had committed a foul stench. And so, with this story so known, the husband stayed home from then on. And the wife, she got her way.

Well, since I started telling you this story, none of you have claimed distaste for the way I was raised. And none of you seem so dull as to not know, which must mean you know I'm a wise woman, and do not care.

Do they have women like me in your village? Someone with the knowledge of how to take what may look like a bundle of different weeds and herbs, and turn it into something that could save your life, or take it. And I don't mean to boast, but I don't exaggerate when I say wise. Between you and me, I believe myself to be the only person left with any sense at all in these parts!

You have wise women in your village, then? Have you no priest? They too do you no good. The priest in our village - the priest in <u>the</u> village - he's an ageing man now, but I remember when he first came. While we lived in the village still, my mother and I, again many years ago. You wouldn't know to look at him now, but he was handsome once. He wasn't rough like the other men of the village were rough. He spoke nicely, he was learned, lettered and when first he came, his one mission seemed to be to win over my mother. And I may have been a tiny thing, but I had eyes in my head. When he thought none were looking, the glances he would give my mother. The conversations they would have, going on for hours on into the night and early morning: he desperate to win her over to the cause of this new god and she desperate to only get him to eat something, for he was skinnier than having past three winters with a bare cupboard. I wonder sometimes if she hadn't put something special in what she tried to make him eat, for it was plain she thought him well too, but I don't think it was needed. He never gave anyone as much attention as she. It became the talk and stuff of song near us: 'The Priest That Loved The Wise Woman'. And for a little time, it was overlooked. Accepted. Even thought nicely of.

But then…some time passed and another priest came and stayed a while with ours. The priest brought us to meet him, and the look this stranger priest gave to us. He bent down to me and asked: 'Where is your father, child?'

None other spoke as I said back to him: 'I have no father, sir. Never had.' And he looked up at my mother then as if he might kill her where she stood.

The stranger priest stayed a while, and then, after he had left again… Our priest would walk past us in the road with never a glance in our direction. He never came to see us anymore. He would still watch my mother sometimes, from the other side of the way, or from where he thought she could not see, but then he would look away when he saw I saw him. I don't know who was more hurt, my mother or he. Fool. To let what someone else has told him decide how he finds his happiness? Silly Christian fool.

I did miss him, though. Once he'd decided we were not to be spoken to. I have very fond memories of the times he would spend in our house, him sitting me on his knee before the fire and then, as always, I would beg my mother to tell us the stories of her mother. Her grandmother. Their mothers before them. How The Old Wolfskin that my mother wore had been passed from mother down to daughter, to carry on what had been taught and learnt before. My mother knew of things that she and her mothers had done. Looked to find things that had not yet happened. Healed those sick or in need. They all did things to appease the gods of the forest and the waters and the lands to influence a bountiful harvest and an easy winter. She told me of times past – a time when we were truly loved.

We were the central part of our community. Not just my mother and hers. Wise women. Cunning women. The things that we did ensured a people prospered and they would not do without us. No village survived without us and for it, they carried us on their shoulders on holy days. They strung flowers through our hair and had us bring them together and bless them, their unions, their children. They called our names and sang songs of us and we were always welcome in another's house, we had friends, we were brought food, we were always kept the best place for by the fire, even in the coldest winter...

Those are the stories I was told, anyway. I've no such memories.

I cling to those stories, because I must. I've never known that and I don't think my mother did. Just the tales. So many tales. But it's important to remember stories of the past. As my mother's mother would say: 'How can you tell where you are, if you don't cast a look behind you now and again?'

No one to cast a look back with though now, is there? Look. All the women of my family dedicated to that village and what's it purchased us? This. A place thrown together in the middle of the woods, and none to visit us unless they must.

I've told you, no – there's no man here. Gave up the idea of finding one long ago. Never even been touched. Well, nearly. But I am fair glad it never came to pass.

Eadwine his name was. You go on into the village tomorrow, and if he still lives, you'll meet him or hear him talked about. He has the larger of the homes you'll see. His wife is plain, younger than him, weak little thing, does as she's told. Never seen her smile, but she never did me any harm... But Eadwine...

"Maya. I brought this for you. I thought you - and you mother - might have need of it. Thank you for the remedy you gave Hild, she fairs much better than she did... I wish I could thank you in deed as through speaking. You are so lovely. Lovelier even than your mother."

'Thank you for this. I'll make sure my mother gets it.'

It went on for months. Every day, almost, there was some excuse for him to come by our house. Hild was ill again. Hild did not sleep well, and needed something to help her. Hild slept too much and needed something to wake her. I began to wonder if it would not be kinder to just kill Hild, for how ill she always seemed to be. But Eadwine was always there, at the door, staring in. Telling me how lovely I was when my mother was not there. How he liked my mouth and the shape I was taking as I grew. I never knew what he meant, of course. I was barely so high as his elbow. I was always nice, but soon, of course, his speech changed.

"Maya, you tell me true: have you placed some curse on me? If you have, I will forgive you, but you must take it off. I cannot love my wife, but for thinking of you. And yet, I know the cure, you see! To take the curse off again, you must see out the visions you have put with me. You must lie with me so it may pass, but you cannot leave me like this. Have some pity, Maya. You'll be good to Eadwine, won't you?"

I had no need for cursing, of course. And if I were to ever make a love hex, a man of gold would not satisfy me. I'd have chosen a man far younger, with less fat around his middle, less years about his face and far less wife back at home. And then one day, he seems to be a man gone wild. He starts to grab at my hands, tries to make me touch him. So I scream, just the once. My mother knows I scream for nothing, and into the house she comes, as Eadwine presses himself atop me.

My mother's voice was like the cold steel of a resting sword. "You'll leave off my daughter, Eadwine. Get off her, and you'll not be sorry."

He laughs in her face. "You'll not stop me, old woman!" and he starts to pull at his clothes.

"No," she says, "you're too strong for me. But I'm sprightly enough. Will you be done before I can run and fetch your wife, to bring her so she sees what you do when you cannot lie with her? Will you be finished before I go and fetch Hild's father? Now there is a bear of a man; and here he'll see how you disregard his only child. Will you be done by the time I've gone to fetch the priest to let him know what you do when you do not go to hear him bleat?"

We all were now still, all three of us, for what seemed like all time, as if none of us might ever move again. Then, as if nothing had happened in the first place, Eadwine got to his feet, took himself through our door, and was gone. My mother and I still moved not at all for some time 'til we were sure he would not come back.

And come back, he never did. He never came to the house again. From time to time, our eyes would catch in the street, but then he'd look away and never meet my gaze. And I cannot tell you why, but even now, that pleases me.

...Why should I talk on such things?! It's been so long since I had real visitors here - not like when I was younger. Things have changed for me indeed. You see, many, many years ago, when the Christians came to this place; they brought with them their coin, bearing the faces of he who owned them all on it. And it's said that, at first, they preached peace between us all. There was no need to fight about what was believed between us. Their God didn't like fighting. Sounds like a pretty poor God to me, if he doesn't enjoy a good fight, now and again!

Everyone has fought. We fight between the villages, about boundaries and land that one can grow good food in, or graze our animals in. We fight in the square, about prices, about what's mine and what's not yours, or even in playing games with each other. Brothers fight. That's why the strongest of us stay alive. Because life is a fight at times, and those that live have learnt to fight, and fight well.

But the Christians didn't fight. No. What they did…That wasn't fighting. That was something different, and we didn't know it until too many years had passed for us to see… The Christians planted seeds.

You know how seeds work? You sow a seed, you wait. You water it, you wait. You let the sun shine on it, you wait. They planted seeds in people's minds, a seed that blossomed into this idea of a world where we all go once we have passed out of this life, and though we cannot see it, hear it, smell taste it or hold it, it was a terrible thing to think otherwise. That rather than the gods of the land, the ancient gods, the gods we knew and loved and who looked after us, that there was only this One God. God of everything, all lands. I mean – does it not sound like madness? One God looking after all you see? All things?

My mother and I never thought of it at the time, even as the chapel in the village was built. What was it to us, what other people wanted to think and believe? We knew what we knew, and we worked by that. So, we did nothing.

Then with the years passing as I grew towards womanhood, we heard our own village folk talking of it. They spoke words that could not have been theirs, and said things to us of things they could not know, as if they knew better than we! And we came to realise that instead of sitting at our fires and telling us their stories and listening to ours, they had been going to see this priest and listen to his words. And suddenly, we, following what we had been taught, the stories of our mothers, the ways in which to make a village prosper…

I couldn't understand it. So do you want to know what I did?

One day, I snuck into the chapel. I wanted to understand. I stood at the back so none would pay too much mind by me. People gathered and waited, and gossiped, and then the priest arrived, and began to speak, and the chapel was silent but for his voice. I barely recognized him as he spoke. He stood in front of all, and in a voice not quite his own, he spoke. He promised all who heard him what we've never known before: A life without toil. Never wanting for anything. This beautiful, happy place where there is no fear, no hunger, or sickness, or dying. And to come by such a place, and spend forever there without leaving, there was so little that was asked in return. He spoke so passionately about it, I almost believed him.

But then I looked about me. All who stood in the chapel listened, eagerly, their faces lit with joy and hope. But - what had they show for these promises? Their lives were no better today, not tomorrow, nor had been since their first hearing of these words. And yet, they all believed it! It came to me, as I listened on, now watching all the folk that I knew so well, that they wished to believe it. That it was all, indeed, the best promise that had ever been made to them since they emerged from their mothers' wombs. Perhaps even the priest himself had wanted so hard to believe it that he'd forgotten a time when he hadn't.

But I am not so easily sold on promises. Not the promises of men who sneak through everywhere, steal the holy days of the ancient gods and bastardise them into their own twisted purpose. For what? So that simple-minded folk'll pay over what they've scraped and struggled already to get so that this one man, who has never been to our land, can keep in wine and fine clothes? I remember what the priest told me and my mother over our broth when I was young, I knew. Yet them that stood about me, they didn't see that. They hear this man's word and they trust him! It's so easy and good to hear that burdens will be lightened, that they don't ask even for proof. They'd rather listen to stories of something that happened far away, long ago, in a different land to different people, than listen to their own stories of their families, those that went before them, the people who fought and struggled and survived, their own history.

I told some of what I'd heard to my mother. I should not have done that. I spoke of it while we were without the house. I should not have done that.

"Enemy?" she said. "They say the likes of me is an Enemy? I've never met this God, so how can I be his enemy?' I told her to hush, but she wouldn't listen. She turned to those who stood about us and asked aloud: "Why do you put your faith in a man who tells you of these lovely things, denied you until you're in the mud, when he hasn't met this God either? He repeats what he's been told, same as me and my daughter, but we give you things in your hand, we turn a good season, we do things you can see. What has this God done that I can see, except turn good people from their sense, and into all these sheep they talk so much of?!"

That was when we lived in the village. Many seasons ago now. Our house in the village once bustled with activity. People here and there, talking with each other, getting advice, giving it, drinking, eating, even singing old songs, all together, all at once... But now we were never visited. Now we were alone. People only came to us when they were sure they would not be found out for it. It's a wonder their mothers and fathers before them don't all rise from their graves and shake some sense into the people of that village. Sometimes I reckon on putting on my mother's Old Wolfskin and going out to call them forth!

Yet I know it's not the same all over. It's not like this everywhere. There's another village my mother would take me to when I was very young. The wise woman there, she and my mother were friends. There, they never had a priest. They listened to the old wisdom and the old gods. Our priest went there once and from what I heard, was sent away with no vagueness in his ear or on his backside about how they felt about the new god! The wise woman, the village comes to her with everything. First crops to ask the blessings for the season. A sheep or a goat whenever she has need of one. If there is something wrong in her house, why it is the village that comes in and puts it right. They look after her, because they know she looks after them.

And here, they scorn me. Sometime ago, I had need to go into the village, and there I went, and as I stood to buy something, I felt all at once something warm and wet on the back of my legs and when I turned, a man, a man I knew and once would have called a friend...more than friend one time, I hoped... had loosed himself and pissed all over me. Everyone who saw laughed, or hid their faces. I felt my face flush red. I didn't even stay to buy what I needed. I went straight out into the stream, walking into it and I sat there in the icy water, shaking from the cold for what seemed to be hours, trying to get rid of the stench as it clung to my clothes, clung to my skin, that horrible warm wetness that I couldn't shift!

After a time, when the cold had gotten into my very bones, it was then I realized that it wasn't the stink of piss I was trying to rid myself of. By this time, it was gone. It was shame. It was sorrow. Both clung to me and weren't letting go, and not even running water could wash them away. I did nothing wrong! Nothing!

It's been so long since I felt any kindness now. Not from anyone in the village in a long time. Though... There was a young man, blew through the village like the wind, he did, years ago now. Dunstan was his name.

"Hello? Is there any here?" comes his voice.

'There is,' says I. 'I don't know you. What do you want?'

"I was...told I should come here if I were a man with a problem," says he.

'Who told you that? And besides, every man has a problem. His chief one being that he is a man.'

"Aye," he laughed. "Aye, they said you were sharp-tongued. You must be Maya, the daughter, have I got that right? Forgive me - they said that you could help me, they did not say… You are a handsome woman."

'I know,' says I. 'I've also much to do. What is it that you want?'

"My problem is sleep," he confides. "I cannot. Not for months now. I sometimes sleep when darkness comes, but never 'til the sun rises again, and sometimes not at all. What can I do?'

'Have you tried rolling over your wife when she snores?' I ask.

"I, er… I don't have a wife."

'Ah,' I speak. 'That problem is the greatest of them all.'

"I've not yet taken a wife," he tells me quickly. "I'm a merchant, I'm a travelling man. Though I might like to think of it, I cannot be at home with a wife all the time."

'Well if it brings you any peace,' says I with a smile, 'for such, you sound like the ideal husband to me.'

"Is that even so?" says he, and he looks about the house, with a smile that dare not show its face proper yet. "Is it, er, just you and your mother here, then?"

'It is,' I reply, myself with a smile. 'I've no husband to keep awake with my sharp tongue.'

"That cannot be right. I know men as'd give part of themselves to be kept awake all night by a tongue like yours."

Now there are many things that I have heard the village boys say, but not strangers, I think, so I take what he needs and thump it into his hand. 'Take this Valerian and some chamomile! If you still cannot sleep now, it's no fault of mine!'

He looks like a stupid man into his own hand. "How shall I pay you?" he asks.

'Just don't come back,' says I, and I turn my back to him.

He is quiet for some time, then: "I'm sorry, I have offended you."

'You offend me more by staying,' says I with a whirl. 'What woman wants a man? What man wants a woman more than what he can get out of her?'

"Now, that's not true!" says he, his voice raised. "I had a woman I wanted for my wife, but she died!"

I saw in his face that this was the truth and instantly was aggrieved for speaking. 'I'm sorry for it. When was this, when you were younger?'

"No," he says with difficulty. "Near the same time I stopped sleeping… You've got a fire in you," he says with a saddened grin as he looks at me. "So did she. Women with real fire, like yours… If this does not work," he says of the herbs, "next time I come through, may I come back to you?"

'They will work,' I say. 'But very well.'

As thought this does not satisfy him, he tarries a while, then says at last: "If next time I come through and I can sleep… may I still come back to you?"

I cannot look to him to let him see me smile. 'As you like, I suppose. I'm not a woman that can be bought, though.'

"I can tell so - that's why I ask. What I mean to say is - if next time I come, if you've still no husband to keep awake… I'm sure we could find good excuses to not sleep."

'I don't know you,' I say, the breath gone from my voice.

"And marriage is the best excuse to get to know each other that I can think of. Look, I must pay you for this. I've a wagon outside. It's full of cloth. Worth a lot. You'll see it on the back of a king someday. Go outside and get as much out of it as you can carry. That can be your payment.'

I stare at him. 'Why are you doing this?'

"Because I think we both be lonely."

'...When might you be back?' I dare to ask.

"Not before next season. Can you wait that long?"

He was the kindest as any had been to me in a long while. Fashioned this cloak from the beautiful cloth he had. Is it not the finest thing you ever saw?

Best I never knew what happened to him. He might have found himself a wife back home. He might have forgotten all about it. Or the winter may have got him. I've known men younger and more healthy even than he, struck down in long, harsh winters such as these. Then there's the wolves.

That village of mine. They'll regret it someday! In front of everyone else, they treat me with scorn. They'll call me evil things and tell me to get gone. But! - when they've a problem – it's not the priest they go to. No man of this new God can cure a festering wound or give relief to a slight woman what is giving birth to a fat child or give a man what he needs to keep his family free from sickness. Sometimes, of course, they go to the priest first. And the priest says some words in this language that we don't even know over them, prays to his god and then - he sends them on their way! With assurances that God will save Them! And then, when they don't get better...I hear a knock on my door.

"Please, Maya, we've already been to the priest and nothing has changed! Work your magic, Maya, take the affliction from us, Maya, stop this pain, Maya, take it from me, please!"

And what can I do? Send them away? Just because of my pain? My mother never turned a man in need away and neither will I.

Sometimes, when they come, it's already too late. Once, this older man came to me with his wife. She'd fallen on a sickle as she worked in the fields, this great gash of blood across her stomach. He'd taken her to the priest at first, and he spoke to God aloud in front of them, laid his hands upon her - "The Christ Jesus will take this from her and make her well again!"

Two days later, they're at my home, begging me. It hasn't gone away. It's gotten worse. It seeps blood and yellow, and I could smell the rot as I opened the door. She could barely stand and her face was white.

I brought her in and seated her, and tried at what I could, then took her husband to the side and said to him:

'It's too late. There's nothing I can do now. Look at her. Why did you not come to me sooner? She needed covering, good covering for it. She needed rest, I bet you've had her up and back in the fields. She needed this washing - I'd have helped her and given something for her pain, but – this! This I cannot cure. This is too far. Why did you not come here first?'

And he says to me: "Maya…we want to go to this Paradise. We work and toil and fear and all is struggle, and we've nothing. We're old now. God took all six of our children, one by one. The only thing we have is the promise that one day, our pains will be soothed and all of this will be for something."

I said: 'The dreams they've sold you. I hope they're worth it in the end.' And I sent them away with a bottle of something I promised would help a little. With the pain, perhaps. But there's nothing could turn that flesh back from its fester. You can't cut away someone's stomach. They buried her in that 'graveyard' they've got by the church.

My mother dead now too. Three winters back. She grew old so quickly after we came to live out here, but it was so much to build a house here. She needed me to remind her sometimes of the very things she had taught me. She'd do a thing and then some little time later, she tried to do it again, as if it had not already been done. She slept longer, and it was the first time I'd really seen her as if she were the age she was. She couldn't walk half so fast. She was fearful if someone came to the door, instead of unafraid as she used to be. But always, she rose before me and sang in the morning. And then, one morning, I awoke to silence.

I buried her myself. Hard work, but I've had harder. On the edge of the glade back there - perhaps you saw it on your way here. She'd sit there and try to listen to the old gods sometimes. I had to bury her deep to be sure the wolves wouldn't smell and come get her…

Somehow word got to the priest that she had died and he came to see me. He promised me that if I went with him then, and told him about all the bad things, the things against 'the Lord' that I had done, then he wanted her buried by the church, and he'd give her a rites or something, so we could all mourn her passing as all the people had loved her, despite the fact she was a heathen woman.

I looked him in the face and told him: Thank You, but why did he think I would go and speak words I didn't mean just so my mother could be put in different earth? Didn't matter to her now, did it? And he walked away. It must have pained him. I've never seen a man walk so slow...

I forget why I stay sometimes. Sometimes I say to myself: Enough. Enough now. Now I go. And I should, find somewhere else, maybe a village without one of these churches and chapels, where they still remember what's important, but…I won't go. I know I won't. Every time I say it to myself, someone comes out of the village, needing help. And they remind me. And though they don't know it, these people do need me. Where would they go, if I weren't here? Where would they take their coughing children? Their parents in pain? To the priest, for his words of comfort? Comfort is little in comparison to herbs that ease the pain and erase the problem. And these priests know nothing of it. I can't leave them. My mother wouldn't have left.

And I wish, sometimes, that the gods had given me a gift. Any gift. Anything to prove myself to them. To the priest. To my mother. To myself. Any gift. Do you hear me?

*

Oh! Yes. Yes of course I remember you. Forgive me - I didn't think there'd be anyone coming through 'til at least spring. I'm glad to know you got there well enough. Was there plenty of food? Did you bring any back with you? My stores are a little bare these days…

I don't think you should stay here tonight. We had a good dinner last time together and your company was very welcome but…I can't let you stay again. You're better off going onto the village. There may even be work there for you now, should you want. They've lost some hands, you see, they'll probably be very grateful of extra help…

It's their own fault. It's all their own fault.

That village. Those people. The way they act, you'd imagine they'd be sent into this fiery hell of theirs just for looking at me. Last when I had to buy goods, one of them spat in my open palm. Told me my money was from the devil, and he could not take it for fear of being in league with him.

I said: 'You're talking nonsense! This money - it's all I am left now when I help another. I can tell you exactly who gave me this coin, if it helps you, but it's not from any devil. It's from me. You have known me since you and I were children, what has changed?' But then he ignored me. Wouldn't even let me have the goods I'd come to buy. I appealed to his wife, but she ran back indoors at the very sight of me.

Part of me thinks it must be my fault. I should have just taken a lover long ago, had a daughter of my own, passed all the secrets that I knew onto her, but… As soon as the winter has passed… I go.

I wasn't going to. But something happened. Had it not, I'd probably still try and fool myself that I was needed, that I should stay, but not now. I cannot possibly stay now.

Where to begin? You swear to me that what you hear from me, you will never say to another, until you know me dead, or you take it to the grave yourself. I mean it! I can curse you if you break your word and trust me, the costs for crossing me will not be light…

I cannot even say what made me leave the house that night. It was bitter cold. I had nowhere to go and no business being out so late, but…I wrapped myself up in my mother's old wolfskin for warmth and then, my feet just took me past my front door and out on into the woods. Maybe it was the loneliness, maybe it was something else…

There was a frost covering the land. I stayed away from the path, even though I knew this to be dangerous, the icy ground crunching beneath my feet. I walked on until I came to the edge of the wood, and in the moonlight, I could just make out the village, snatches of laughter and merriment from them inside their warm houses reaching me. Firelight shining from under doors and smoke through chimneys.

Warm and safe and happy and together, I thought. Happy to piss on me when it was my family what kept this village together. What saved those who would otherwise have died in harsh, long winters such as these. And what do me and my mother have for it? She gone, when she might have had many years left to her; and me, all alone. Friendless. Having to till my earth and soil and hunt for myself and guard myself from others until I'm too old and weak to stand, and then to waste away within my own home and no one will even know I'm gone or shed tears or bury me or remember my name. And this hatred and anger built up within me, and as I pulled my mother's wolfskin around me even tighter, I whispered:

'I'll see blood for what you've done to us.'

I should have remembered my mother words in that moment. I asked her once why she did not speak foul of those that treated her so badly, when I could see the rage within her. And she told me: "My daughter, never say a word against a living man if you are flush with anger. When passion runs that high, you can be sure the gods will hear you."

No sooner had I spoken my words, than this howl drifted out of the darkness, out of the wood behind me. Long and high. And I recognised it. It was the howl they made when they were beginning a hunt. But that could not be right. The wolves had never come this close to the village before. And fear struck me. It was winter, and it was so cold, and the frost seemed to have lasted forever… They must be hungry, I thought, starving out there, what with all the rest of the world asleep all around them and for a moment – a terrible moment – I became so afraid for the words I'd spoken. For if my mother was right, and the wrong words are heard by those that ought not to be listening… Not the good gods. Not the benevolent. Not those that watch and wait in quiet while we all make fools of ourselves. There are other things too. Things that love the darkness, love death, love the chance to flex themselves when one calls for them but knows it not…

I tell myself I didn't have time to run to the village. What wise woman can tend a village if she's dead? So I ran to the first tree that I could scale, and I climbed as far and as high as I could, climbed far out of reach, and peered down through the branches.

And suddenly, there they were. So many of them, more than I'd ever seen before, more than I could count. Thin and unhealthy, and looking so hungry. Yet still so large and terrifying, their teeth like scythes, glinting like the frost all around. They stared towards the village for a moment, as I had done. Snarling and growling, this horrible, low noise as I clung to that branch and trembled with the cold and the fear.

Then, as if someone had given a word, they ran! Altogether, all at once, running towards the village. Running towards the smell of cooking meat on open fires. Running towards small children, already weakened by the season. Running towards sleeping, unknowing people, lying in their beds. And all I could do from where I was, was watch and listen.

They ran so fast, it seemed their paws never touched the ground, ran in among the houses and the buildings, the snarls and the growls getting louder, turning to barks and bays, loud and horrible. More and more joining, as so many wolves overran the village. And then - oh, then - suddenly - I hear human cries! Terrified children and desperate maids and helpless men, shrieks and screams of fear and agony and desperation, fighting for their lives, things being thrown, doors being smashed, and panic and voices I almost recognised, words I could almost make out, sounds of gargling and snapping and tearing, and the frost played tricks on my eyes as I thought I saw a dark, blackened pool creep out onto the path…And I put my hands over my ears and I shut my eyes as tight as they could go and I clung to the branch with my legs and I lay there in quiet and cold, for I could do nothing!

And…

The night went by. After some time, there was a single howl. I waited. Then the wolves began to disappear back into the woods, following each other back into the darkness. Only one of them saw me - the last out of the village that I saw. Enormous and dark, eyes like fire. He came to the trunk of the tree and looked up at me. Placed his forepaws on the bark and just looked right at me. Blood all over his snout. But it wasn't in hunger he seemed to look at me. It was as if he was trying to tell me something.

'No!' I said, as if he might understand me. 'This was not what I wanted…'

He stayed a moment, then ran after his brothers into the woods. I climbed down…

And I came home. Pretended I'd never even been out. Sleep did not come easy. I was almost able to tell myself it must have been a dream.

Then in the morning came the knocks. People came, many, to fetch me for their family, their neighbours. Tears and fear on their faces. Many had died. Some were nearly dead. Some died in my arms. All were terrified. Those few unharmed went about putting the people into the graveyard, and the wolves were buried at the edge of the forest. Everywhere was a mess. My cheeks flamed red as I walked through and I tried… I tried not to think that it was me that caused it. How do I know it was? But even worse, there were times I had to struggle not to smile. *How does it feel,* I wanted to say. *How does it feel to know how powerless you can be?* I made them feel it…

But now I tried to put it right. I did what I could. I gave potions, I bandaged, I gave advice, I washed them… And nearby, suddenly I heard the priest. He called so loud it was as if he wanted his God to hear him.

'Look at where your ungodliness has brought you! This village of sin. This is

God's work and it was right we be punished. We have allowed ourselves too much for too long and suffered those who would send us to Hell to live far too long!'

I didn't stay after that. People started whispering. Looking in my direction. I heard my name. I knew it best not to stay. I've seen them afraid, but never this afraid. Fear, when it is put in one place, among many people, can be more deadly than what made the people fearful first.

So. As soon as the winter's passed, I'll leave. I've no choice now. I've no notion where to go, either, but if even one person saw me that night…

Do you want to know what happened today? I was putting things in order in my house, not long before you came, when a knock came on my door. I answered it. It was a man wounded. One of the wolves had sunk its teeth so deep in his arm; there was a part where you could have seen bone. Didn't smell right. He stood on my threshold, cradling his wounded arm like it was a young baby.

"Please, Maya. You must help me. The blood still comes and will not stop, but it brings water too. It aches so much I cannot sleep, and cannot keep down what I eat. Please, Maya, give me something to make this wound go away!"

I opened my mouth to tell him come in, let me see to it… But then I looked a little closer and I recognized him. I knew him. I once might have called him friend. But in that moment, my pride took over me, reminded me of my heart full of sorrow and shame, that day in the village, going to sit in the stream all by myself…So I said to him: "You could try pissing on it. That's what you do when you want something to go away, isn't it?"

And for the first time, though perhaps it hurt me as much as it was hurting him, I shut my door. On someone who needed me. I heard him cry as he left. I don't know if it was in pain or in fear, but I'll never forget the sound of that man's tears 'til I'm in my grave. I wanted to go out and call him back and tell him to come back in; of course I'll help, because that's what I do…. But I couldn't. And I didn't.

Where is it that you said you came from? Your village? Is it far? Would it be so long to walk? I reckon that all us walking together might stave off the cold somewhat. I'd be no trouble. I'd keep pace. I can help along the way. Perhaps I could… Maybe I can… Take me with you. If I don't go, then everything, my mother's words, all the work of her mothers, what has happened here, it'll be lost. They don't care about old stories unless it leads to something good for themselves anymore. You can't let it be lost. Let me come with you.

Please?

Mrs. Oscar Wilde

Introduction

After *The Witch In The Woods*, I focused on short film and after producing *Learning To Talk* which has, to date, garnered a good number of awards and nominations. I wasn't, however, particularly thinking of doing another one woman show any time soon. I self-consciously dipped my toe in the water of where else might take a show like *TWITW*, but I was not actively looking. By chance, I went to review a show in Burnham Library on the outskirts of Slough & Windsor, which was called *Tea With Oscar Wilde*.

The show itself was light-hearted. The actor Jonathan Goodwin played Oscar Wilde himself, while the show was designed as a chat show in which Oscar invited friends of his such as Lillie Langtry, Marie Lloyd and William McGonagall to converse with him, and the whole theme was one of comedy and fun. I spent the whole time pondering about Oscar. In this particular show, Goodwin played Oscar as openly camp, teasing to the point of being almost raucous, and treating his sexuality as if it were an open and accepted secret.

One of my favourite books from university was Mr. Wilde's one novel: *The Picture Of Dorian Gray*. I read it from cover to cover more than once, and I distinctly remembered reading that Oscar Wilde was not only married, but had children.

Who was this woman, then, who was married to this man who was, to our modern, reflective knowledge, so very known to be a homosexual? A crime that was severely punishable, as was his and his family's undoing?

There is very little one can specifically find written about Constance Lloyd, whom married Oscar in her twenties while his star was still on the ascent. She was, in fact, everything the sensationalist Victorian celebrity could have hoped for in a wife: intelligent, pretty, from a good family, a feminist (as was Oscar himself), hardworking, an avid writer and able to carry the mantle of celebrity that her union with Oscar offered her with great aplomb and grace. She and Oscar were, for over a decade, The Celebrity Couple, the Victorian Posh & Becks, if you like. She did not shrink into the background, merely to be a coffer for her husband through her inheritance, and despite long-term ill health, life-long shyness and some incredibly unsettling experiences in her youth, she was one of the most well-known and respected women of her age.

It felt somehow wrong that, given that she was as much a part of Oscar's star as the likes of Bosie, Oscar's long-term lover, more was not generally known of her. I thought little of it until I had the following conversation:

> Me: I wish I could write a play about Mrs. Oscar Wilde.
> Them: Weren't that a man?
> Me: No, he was married. To a woman.
> Them: Well, I suppose they had to in their day!
> Me: ... Actually from what I can tell so far, he might not have thought or felt he was gay when they were first married.
> Them: Oh, so it was her fault then?

I had been given the inspiration to write the play. Now I had a cause.

Constance was, thankfully, an avid letter-writer, which is how we are able to get most of our insight into her life still today. With her being a somewhat modern character (in contrast to anyone pre-Victorian, I mean), there was much more specific information available about her and therefore much more research to be done and facts to be inserted that could paint not only a fuller but more accurate picture of her life.

This observed, I went looking for Constance's voice in her letters and writing, and her personality, for saying she started life as a rather shy young woman, was loud and clear. I decided to put excerpts from letters that she had written into the play itself, so that Constance's voice and words, verbatim in most instances, were at the core of the story - both to her brother Otho, as they are all aimed in the play, and to other friends, such as Lady Mount-Temple, with whom she shared a long friendship. Her own words are marked in italics throughout the play, and there is a bibliography at the back of this book for fans of Constance's, old and new, to refer to.

One of the hottest talking points about Constance and, in particular, the last few years of the Wildes' marriage, is just how much Constance was aware of Oscar's extra-marital affairs with men. It's possible she lived in sublime ignorance until the very moment of his arrest. It's possible she simply thought that any rumours of what might truly be going on between Oscar and Bosie were simply stories made by detractors, jealous of Oscar's success and talent. It's completely possible as well that she eventually became aware of her husband's nature, and tried to simply look the other way until there was no other direction to look. In the play, I pitch it that someone quite as naive and good-natured as Constance on the whole might have such a hard time even thinking of her once-doting husband as a practicing homosexual, that she spends some of the later years of her marriage practically tearing her hair out, trying to figure out exactly what it is that everyone else seems to be aware of, but she is blind to. This is a possibility as plausible as any of the others and, possibly to allow for Constance to rest in peace, the fact is we are unlikely to ever know this particular truth and pain to do with her for sure.

I did have to take certain liberties - or artistic licence as it is occasionally allowed to be called - with elements in the play, mostly to do with the specific timings of events Constance mentions or makes reference to: some events happened a year or more apart, but are mentioned in the same letter for dramatic pacing. It is for this reason that the letters are undated, and rather than mostly taking place on a particular day, are rather to provide a snapshot of Constance's life at that time.

Constance pre-deceased Oscar in 1898, aged only thirty-nine. Her health was in a marked decline in the last few years, and while she is now thought to have been suffering from multiple sclerosis, a little-understood disease in her time, she had two gynaecological operations in the hope of healing herself. She died five days after the latter, possibly of sepsis. She is buried in Genoa, Italy, as Constance Lloyd. The descendants of her brother Otho added the words 'Wife of Oscar Wilde' to her grave in the 1960s.

I hope that, on the whole, *Mrs. Oscar Wilde* is adequate as homage to a forgotten, once-loved celebrity - a woman whose wit not only rivalled her husband, but whose tragic end following a fascinating life of love, betrayal and scandal, was practically made to be told onstage. I hope that in whatever form she may now be understood, she approves. And if she does not, I hope she understands.

WOMEN OF FORGOTTEN IMPORTANCE

Mrs. Oscar Wilde

Dear Otho,

Miss Constance Lloyd present her compliments to Mr. Otho Lloyd & begs to inform him that he has a sister still living.[1]

I'm writing to tell you that it now looks very like, rather than staying with Mama once she has married Mr. King, your sister shall be living either with her Aunt Mary in Norwood in South London, or otherwise at Lancaster Gate with Grandpapa and Aunt Emily. This is all, of course, depending on the marriage actually taking place.

Everything nearly came to a smash…so there was no good in writing till I knew how it was all going to end. I <u>think</u> it is alright, but I do think Mama should have more trust in a man she is going to marry… Mr. SK is charming really & devoted to Mama if only she would see it.[2] Date now set for 19th October and I don't doubt Mama shall want me out of the way before they return from their honeymoon.

Ah well. I suppose, at least, if I am to go, all my 'ugly dresses' of which you complain will be far easier to take than if everything I wore had a bodice with hoops and cages. To answer your question before it is put to me, no, I fear my taste for the Pre-Raphaelite dress, or, to which is now better referred as the 'Aesthetic' style of dress, has in no way waned. While I admit other women may be content to be contorted and look admirable; myself and my friends are far more content to be comfortable, and able to breathe.

I want to know if you got your £10 from Grandpapa & if they told you of the money arrangements. Grandpapa is going to make you quite independent of Mama & to give me an allowance of how much I know not yet. He will not give Mama a farthing, at which she is rabid. Would God I were independent too; I would far rather work for my daily bread than have my mother make a compliment of me keeping me in food and lodging. She says it is grandpapa's duty to keep the children of his only son and she says that his keeping you is no compliment, as if he did, she is no longer bound to keep you, & you would have to leave Oxford and take a clerkship! A nice look-out for the son of Horace Lloyd & for me with abilities like yours too![3]

Otho, when you write to me, you tell me much about your friends at Oxford, but so very little of your studies. As you may suspect, though proud of you beyond measure, my vanity has prompted in me not a little amount of jealousy, to which I readily admit. You see, it is my own desire, my own sincere wish that one day, women shall walk the same halls that you now do; shall be able to count themselves as educated as you soon shall.

I went to see Mr. Morgan yesterday, and he said that I was very weak indeed, with scarcely any pulse… He has given me tonic pills… ordered me to lie down and sleep every day after lunch, all of which Mama pooh poohed and declared it was only indigestion: she asked me if it was her cruel treatment of me that made me weak?! [4]

Your allusion to things past, particularly the behaviour of Mama towards your sister… What can truly be said of it? Who could have thought how she would turn after father's death? I tell myself that the things said, the coldness and cruelty… the threat of fire-irons and having one's head crushed against the wall… These are things that are soon to feel long in the past, and are not to be burdens upon your good person for your inability to prevent them. It was terrifying for the both of us, but I beg we write no more of it. That which cannot be changed must be accepted.

A propos of the honourable lady about to be married, it is necessary we give her a present & that present must be… costly… She has fixed her affections on a plain gold bracelet. I find the smallest to be £7.7.6. [5]

Oh me! When shall I marry me? You say I shall have a chance of marrying. I see none. I have no beauty, no conversation, no small talk even to make me admired or liked… I wish I were anything like some of my friends, able to speak in front of others with ease and wit and grace. But I? *I do think I am the greatest donkey that ever lived, I am so afraid of people. I shall be an old maid, I am doomed to it & you shall see your Sister walking about with 6 cats and half a dozen dogs.* [6]

Yours,

Constance

Postscript:

I did laugh at the wonderful story you related of your Oxford friend going to Greece, arriving back to Oxford a fortnight too late, almost to be sent down by the authorities! But, as to his name, does he belong to the same family of Merrion Square in Dublin? For if so, then surely Grandpapa will know them socially. And I am sure I have heard the name of 'Oscar Wilde' before.

*

My Dearest Otho,

I am so terribly disappointed in your being plucked... It cannot but force itself upon my mind, seeing Grandpapa's disappointment, almost unspoken, it is true but scarcely for the less, that you have not worked, or you have only indolently as we are both only too inclined to do. Do dear boy try and make up this future year and work steadily and try to attain the honours that I know with study you have the capability of attaining...

Do not think I am lecturing you. You know that all my ambitions, my future hopes are bound up in you and it is really a keen disappointment to me to see that you have none for yourself and it is not only that, but it is Grandpapa's money that is being spent and if you do not profit by your college career it is wasted, is it not so?

Is there any possible way by which I can help you? Remember that ignorant as I am, I will do anything in my power, or learn anything by which I could afford you any possible assistance.[7]

For me to go any further into my disappointment in this matter, Otho, for myself as well as for my fear for you, I regret will bring me to tears. You have been afforded all that one may needed in order to affect a great start in life - position, education, breeding, family, gender....

Please, darling, consider this if nothing else. A little toil is so very worth it in the end.

Yours in faith,

Constance

*

Dearest Otho,

I write to you having now long returned from Holland to England, and from my holiday with Aunt Emily and Grandpapa. Surely expect me to regale you with tales from this holiday, but I fear I must unburden myself of what happened before we even set sail. While we waited to board the ship, Uncle Charlie and Cousin Stanhope joined us there quite by chance... Or I took it to be so much.

Otho. *Did it ever in your wildest dreams enter your head that Stanhope cared for me? I went out for a long walk with him... and he informed me that he had come to ask me to be his wife.*[8] As if that were not so bad, I found, to my astonishment that our 'fortune' in crossing paths was nothing of the sort. It was all arranged and all the family knew of it. All but I. *I do hope no one again will ever propose to me for it is horrid. He said… he would have waited to test my feelings but that our going away tomorrow had hurried him on. It was so dreadful. I could but refuse him and he came again* [the next morning] *to get a final answer and looked white as a sheet and frightened me so and yet I could not do anything else, could I? He would insist that I cared for someone else, and I assured him I did not. I sent him away, and I don't want to marry, and I do hope nobody else will ever ask me. I am shaking all over still with* [9] the mere memory of it.

However, even since our return to England, I seem also to have acquired the admiration of another gentleman. His name is Mr. Fitzgerald. *Deep sigh. He requested to escort me somewhere this week. It ended finally in his arranging to come to Devonshire Terrace* [to take] *Mama, Ella, Tizey and myself to the Fancy Fair at the Albert Hall… Poor man. I left Zena and him to have a long conversation together but he made his way over after a time and I couldn't get rid of him. [He] was with me the whole afternoon and to my horror, I positively loathe him now … Isn't it horrid?* [10]

I was worried I should never get married once upon a time, but nowadays I fear it may be being orchestrated beyond all my control. *I have no special objection to being married, excepting that I don't care for anyone and that I think I am rather afraid of marrying.*[11]

I am glad Aunt Ella is taking me to a tea party in Devonshire Terrace tomorrow. It seems that Grandma Atkinson has decided that, at 29, the situation is becoming desperate and Ella must be married immediately. She has it in mind to match-make her with a young man you'd probably know from your Oxford days. He's a poet, though if he is the same gentleman I am thinking of, then I have seen more of the derivatives of him they have made in the newspapers than his work. He's apparently a peculiar gentleman, but meant to be quite brilliant, and celebrated for his honest opinion.

If I were to ever marry, it would have to be someone brilliant; I couldn't bear the thought of outstripping my husband in wit. How awful that would be…

Tear up this letter.[12]

Constance.

*

Dear Otho,

I'm sure I need not make it too plain that what I write of here, while all is in the balance, must be disclosed to no one. I beg, not even your wife.

You may recall that I detailed in a previous letter, my intent to attend the tea party at Devonshire Terrace Grandmama was hosting. When I arrived, I soon found myself sitting next to a tall gentleman, who, on learning my name, expressed interested in our Irish connection. He himself was Irish also. He complimented me on my dress, that which you would have thought was ugly, and then, we talked. Of everything, all matters. Of art, literature, of the female role in society - and I found his ideas refreshingly similar to my own!

All the while we spoke, other guests of the party seemed to hover about us, like bees about honey, but all the while, we spoke with each other alone. I felt inexcusably rude and yet, I found it almost impossible to care!

Eventually, of course, it came time for him to leave. As he rose to go, he turned to me and said he had enjoyed our conversation very much, and that he hoped we have chance to meet again very soon to continue it. I tried to remain as proper as possible, but I confessed I felt very much the same. As he turned to leave, every head turned to watch him make for the door.

Grandmama was sitting opposite me and when the door shut behind the gentleman, she inclined slightly towards me and said 'My dear, you don't know who that was, do you?'

I admitted I did not. While the gentleman had seemed somewhat familiar, I was certain I had never met him before. She smiled at me and her eyes seemed to glimmer. 'That is Mr. Oscar Wilde. You've heard of him by now, I'm sure.'

And inexplicably, Otho, the compliment that he had paid me, by spending so much of his afternoon devoted to my company, seemed weightier, while my heart was so much lighter in my chest. I knew at once that he was indeed your friend, from your Oxford days, but it was very difficult for me to connect the two personages in my mind. Mr. Wilde is, after all... Well, he's terribly well-known these days, you know, Otho. He is a writer, and he gives lectures also. He's very well thought of, and has quite a reputation now, though he is perhaps not taken all too seriously, though he seems not to mind that so much, as he himself admitted.

There is more!...There is more...

On the 7th of June, our Aunt Emily held an 'At Home' and who should do you suppose she should invite? Now knowing now who he was, I must admit that I shook with fright on his arrival. Recalling that the original design was for he and my Aunt Ella to form an attachment, I greeted him with:

'My Aunt Ella is not here, I fear to tell you Mr. Wilde. She'll be so disappointed to have missed you.'

To which he replied: "In that case, Constance, I fear you shall have to be the greatest consolation prize that ever a man knew."

He called me by my name. He does everyone, he's frightfully modern, but *…I can't help liking him because when he's talking to me alone, he's never a bit affected, and speaks naturally, excepting that he uses better language than most people.* [13]

Here is the truth of it, Otho. We have met since. We have met many times since! We almost instantly met each other's mothers. I find Lady Wilde a wonderfully fascinating woman to hear speak, and it is from she that Oscar gets his good opinion on the capabilities of women. She writes under the pen name of Speranza back in Ireland, and is frightfully well received.

Though Aunt Emily was scandalised by it, recently, Mr. Wilde took me to the theatre to see Othello - just the two of us, you understand. Afterwards, he asked me if I should be so good as to meet a very great friend of his. He took me backstage and who do you suppose he introduced me too, but Ellen Terry herself!

Grandpapa I think likes Oscar, but of course the others laugh at him, because they don't choose to see anything but that he wears long hair and looks Aesthetic. I like him awfully much, I suppose it is very bad taste. [14]

He is soon to be off to America on his lecture tour. I have known three months of summer to pass like a breath, and yet I worry how long three months coming, where he is so very absent from England, shall seem…

Oh, Otho, I am so very much afraid! What if all of Mr. Wilde's attentions are nothing but a mere dalliance with me on his part? For one need only look into Mr. Wilde's history to see why Mr. Wilde has the reputation that he does. For you know what they say of him. That is a…

You know. That he is…

Oh, must I write the words? That Mr. Wilde is a veritable Ladies' Man.

For after all, one need only look into his recent history to understand why Mr. Wilde has the reputation that he does. Florrie Balcombe, Lillie Langtry, Violet Hunt! How am I ever to compete with these women who have been known to be in his affections? What has made him turn to me?

Please destroy this letter for as you know our family is not over-honourable in such matters as reading other people's letters. [15]

Yours in faith and considerably girlish humour,

Constance

*

Dear Otho,

I wonder that you don't grow tired of my letters. I am almost tired of writing them. But when Grandpapa and Auntie are at home - for you know how Auntie can be especially - I fear there is little for one to do to occupy oneself except to write endless correspondence to one's friends and relations. It always strikes me that our house in Lancaster Gate is so large, and so very nice, but on the whole, if one has not pleasing, stimulating company and people about one, there is so very little to do in it... Auntie has taken to calling me precocious, and she says that I shall make others feel uncomfortable if I continue in this fashion. I did not pay her any mind at first… However, certain things have happened that make me change my mind somewhat, at least...

I am writing mostly because I am quite sure you will find what happened to me recently very amusing. I told you that I was going to Aberdeenshire, did I not? I needed a place in which to sketch for I wanted to complete something for my St. John's Sketch club, and I decided to go and see the Ainslies, at their wonderful home at Delgaty Castle.

I did not anticipate their having a quite full house by the time I arrived, and I met a number of people, some of whom I felt able to talk about my artistic temperament with. One in particular's name was Mr. Huxley. I think he found it rather droll that for every rhetorical question of his, I was able to supply an answer. There was lots to discuss and we spent much time in one another's company, though, as you can imagine, everything was perfectly innocent from both of us. At least, it certainly seemed so, and I meant no harm. I have somewhat missed the ability to speak of certain things in a way that will be understood by the listener.

However, our conversations were not to the liking of another guest, Miss Michelle. She is about forty-five, of Italian descent and is, from what I can tell, still quite unmarried. It took me some little time to realise that she had become frightfully *jealous of me because three days before I came, Mr. Huxley devoted himself to her* [16]... I did not know it, and Mr. Huxley never mentioned it to me, but I do wonder if this, in fact, made it all the worse. *I... offended her mortally and she [would] not forgive me, which [was] rather a nuisance.*[17]

Far from being an end to it, after Mr. Huxley left the castle, it came to my attention, as well as the attention of other guests, that another had decided to take me to his bosom. This person was unfortunately young Master Douglas Ainslie, Mrs. Ainslie's son. The other day, Douglas *began telling me of this scrape he had got into at school and I was advising him - lecturing him he called it, and Miss Michelle who [was] perpetually interfering with everything, went and told Mrs. Ainslie we were in his room together, and so I [was] told I [was] not to go there.*[18] Douglas was upset by this, and confided in me that he had been greatly envious of the attentions I gave to Mr. Huxley during his stay, and had chosen, for whatever reason, to make Miss Michelle his confidante, asking her how he may make himself more agreeable to me. This may well have not greatly appreciated by Mrs. Ainslie, and was likely why she kept so stern an eye turned towards us whenever Douglas spoke to me.

Though my conduct was nothing if not honourable, Douglas is impressionable, somewhat idealistic, and sixteen. Sadly, he did not realise just how obvious his esteem for me was made plain when we were in the company of others, and though I did nothing at all, Mrs. Ainslie became increasingly infuriated with me for apparently flirting with her son. I assured her, this was not the case, not wishing to bring shame to Douglas for his flattering attentions, but it all rather came tumbling down fairly swiftly.

One evening, as I was readying for bed, Mrs. Ainslie came into my room, her face quite puce, and waved some note or other in my face, that had been given to her by Miss Michelle, who had found it. It was Douglas' handwriting and the note, addressed to me, asked if I would be so good as to join him in his room later that evening. Without description of too many unpleasantries, I am now very much back in London, and I got absolutely no sketching done.

Oh, how I do go on. I am sorry, Otho. It is simply that, what both myself and Mr. Wilde initially thought would be a parting for a mere three months, has turned into separation for nigh on a year, his still being in America on his lectures. He still writes to me fairly often, which is how I know that at least, he has not forgotten me entirely. I have no doubt that I shall have very much gone down in his estimations, having been exposed to the exotica of America since we last were in each other's company. I was not so much of a fool to not think that things might still come between us even now. Perhaps you have even heard where you are, the reports that had been made. That Mr. Wilde and the actress Julia Ward Howe's daughter, Maud, had been spending a great deal of time in one another's company. Now that he has come into something of a small fortune, I did not think such reports would be far behind. There were even reports that there was... an understanding between the two. However, Mr. Wilde was very quick to write to me and tell me it was all pure fabrication on behalf of the publication in question.

I have no reason to doubt his good intent, for we are all very much friends here in London now. I see Lady Wilde quite often. I like her dreadfully, for she, just like myself, feels that women have long been overlooked in society and that more must be done to make accommodations for us. She is very inspiring to listen to, and we invariably end our meetings exchanging stories that her son has told us...

Mr. Wilde himself is so very busy though, and doubtless he shall continue to be, even after his return soon... Even after all this time, Otho, I don't think that there is anyone quite like Mr. Wilde. I don't know there ever could be. Perhaps that is the reason why I feel as if I am waiting for him. You will probably think it's all nonsense. The whims of womanly nature! And I will not try to dissuade you. I feel so lacking in vitality at present; I have not the life within me for a disagreement.

I know what else the problem is, however. My purpose feels very murky. I feel that I need some real purpose, and at present I feel I have none. I would ask you to impart some words of wisdom, but I fear to confess that the only person whose words I long to hear just now are Mr. Wilde's. *How can I answer [his] letters? They are far too beautiful for any words of mine. I can only dream of [him] all day long, and it seems as if everyone I meet must know my secret and see in my face how I love [him]...* [19]

I do occasionally catch glimpses of myself in his writing, and wonder if he is, in his own way, simply his own unique self because he feels able to be. If only I were to have an ounce of his confidence. If only I had not been born a woman. And please, do not begin to lecture me in your response that now I must be grateful because finally we are able to own our own property and make use of a bank without the permission of a husband, for, as Lady Wilde might say, a society that is compelled to understand that the female creature, while delicate, is equal in almost every measure to a man, this should have been the case from the start.

At the same time I cannot say that I prefer the life I am leading at present. If I eventually do not marry, I will not live with Auntie all my life. I shall do something. I feel as though I am stagnating and it won't be so bad however if you are in London and I am thinking of going in for an examination. I shan't work my head off for I don't care much about the result. I just want something specific to do to prevent my continually dreaming 'til I get perfectly morbid. [20]

Oh well. The solution will either present itself, or it shall not.

Yours ever,

Constance

*

My dearest Otho,

Prepare yourself for an astounding piece of news! I am engaged to Oscar Wilde and perfectly and insanely happy. [21]

Before you write to ask me if indeed the news be true, I can reveal to you, (the first of many, I am sure), that it is true! Quite true! Though I can barely believe it myself. He wrote and asked me for my hand, and I almost spilled ink all over the return letter in my eagerness to answer him!

I knew I had to write and tell you as soon as possible, for you should be so disappointed to hear it from a pen other than mine. After all, rather soon you should otherwise have heard it announced, as it is to be, in the *Society* and the *Truth* magazines.

My engagement ring is to be quite exquisite. It is of Oscar's own design! Diamonds in the shape of a heart, two pearls within, on a gold band.

Already, we are casting wary glances towards houses that we might like to make our home. *We have been looking at a house in Tite Street which I think we are likely to take.* [22]

I am so dreadfully nervous over my family; they are so cold and practical. I won't stand opposition, so I hope they won't try it. [23] Grandpapa, however, is already withholding his consent, until he feels Oscar has proven that he is in a financial position to keep a wife. But of course he shall be! He made something of a small fortune with his tour of America. He told me that they did not take him altogether seriously in his lectures on Aesthetics, but that his fiscal situation is presently a cause for equal merriment because of it. Then, of course, he continues to speak publically and he is working towards a very serious career in the theatre. Writing, you understand, not being on the stage, though he admits he has not ruled it out.

Oh, Otho! These are nothing but words and details, none of which can convey in this moment the depth of satisfaction and happiness I feel! I wish I could make you understand: I, who thought I should never marry. Never dream to marry one who I considered my equal, my confidante, so great a friend in so many ways. And now Oscar Wilde has asked me to be his. He is everything I could have hoped for in a husband, and yet dared not even hope for it.

I await a returning letter, expressing your astonishment and congratulations.

Yours in abundance of happiness,

Constance

*

Dear Otho,

I have just finished reading your last letter to me.

'If the man were anyone else but Oscar Wilde one might conclude that he was in love. [24] *I don't believe he means anything. That is his way with all girls whom he finds interesting...'* [25]

You must have sent it before I delivered news of my engagement, otherwise I feel sure you would not have written it. I also wonder that, in the circumstance of your having such reservations, that you have waited until now, when it has become quite plain that things were serious between Oscar and myself, and yet you have said nothing before this. I do wonder at it, brother. I understand that your concern is for my good person, but this story about Oscar that you have threatened me with, but have not gone into any detail…

I don't wish to know the story, but even if there were foundations for anything against him, it is too late to affect me now. I will not allow anything to come between us and at any rate no one can abuse him to me… Please for my sake, and because my happiness is dependent upon this thing do not oppose it. [26]

Otho, if you knew what it is to be Oscar Wilde's lover. What it is to be on his arm. How he speaks to me; with more honesty than any other has dared; how he has more daring to be himself than any man – any man – I have ever known. What it is for me to be in his presence, and to be his… If only you understood, Otho, you would agree to never let me know how he may have transgressed when younger. That which has been used against him, or which has been convoluted and twisted to suit the prejudices of those who have neither wit nor person to appear in society as Oscar has established himself. That which I feel certain, even did I know it, and were it true, I would surely be able to forgive him for.

Otho, *I want you now to do what has hitherto been my part for you and make it alright.* [27] I am to be married! Be happy for me, darling!

Yours,

Constance

*

Dear Otho,

Forgive the time it has been since I wrote. I am only just now truly settled at our new abode in Tite Street, and all my things, possessions of comfort and habit, are finally in place.

We were so glad to have you at our wedding, darling. It already seems to long ago, even since our honeymoon in Paris. Did you hear we saw Macbeth while we were there, with Sarah Bernhardt? *The most splendid acting I ever saw. Only Donalbain was bad. The witches, of course, charmingly grotesque. The Macbeth was very good, Sarah, of course superb, she simply stormed the part.* [28]

My dress created a sensation in Paris. Miss Reubell… wants me to get Mrs. Nettleship to make a dress for her exactly like the one of mine. Of course I promised. Imagine Oscar's horrors. [29] Oscar approves of my taste, on the whole, of course. But then he is very much a champion for dresses of sense, comfort and fashion all in one. He knows the dangers of dresses which are all frills and bustles, and are not sensible. Have I told you of his sisters? His father's natural daughters, you know. They died. They two were at a party, and one girl was standing a little too close to the fire. The crinoline of her dress caught alight, then the other girl dashed in to try to put it out... monstrous.

Otho, Oscar's romance knows no bounds. While we were on honeymoon in Paris, we got into something of a routine. He would rise early and venture out with some of his friends, while I would stay behind, but no sooner had he left, than he sent flowers up to the room for me. On his return, he had invariably bought me a gift while out walking. That was how almost all of our mornings went. How charming it was to be courted by Oscar as my lover. How much better it is to be courted by him as my husband. My friend Ada Leverson told me that she believes him *quite madly in love, and [has] showed himself to be an unusually devoted husband.* [30]

Now that I am returned and settled once again in England, I am decided upon joining clubs and societies. I wish to throw myself into it all, as Oscar has done, and I will be ever at his side. The Albemarle – it's a rather famous club, you've probably heard of it - which my husband is already a member of, accepts women. As should all clubs, in my opinion.

I talk of trivialities. Forgive me. I must drop it to express my happiness. It seems that in marrying Oscar, I seem myself to have picked up the mantle of célébrité myself. I have married a man who is not only giving and attentive, but whom cannot go to a single place not be known for who he is.

A few mornings ago, we were taking a constitution about the park, when a gentleman stopped us and spoke to Oscar for something of ten minutes, then tipped his hat politely and went on his way. I had to ask:

'Darling, who was that?'

'I've never seen him before in my life,' said he.

It is quite strange in some ways. I see people glance in our direction, ascertain that it was the Man Himself, the man from the papers, the man of parody, and then they whisper to their friends. 'That's him, isn't it? Yes - that's Wilde. And look there. That must be his wife.'

No one has ever looked at me like that. And now, I find myself on Oscar's arm. Everyone likes him, even those that don't. It is quite delicious to know that every woman in London, whether she admits it or not, would gladly change places with me. Whatever did I do to deserve to be here, I wonder? I wonder if I shall pay for it one day... But that is my mother speaking as much as myself.

We have had to part only once since our wedding. Otho, he wrote to me such words of love.

'I feel your fingers in my hair and your cheeks brushing mine. The air is full of the music of your voice, my soul and body seem no longer mine, but mingled in some exquisite ecstasy with yours…. I feel incomplete without you.' [31]

It feels incorrect to breathe without him. Are you yet happy for me, darling? I have never known joy like this. I never dared think I would.

Yet now I come to the main point of my letter, for I delight to tell you, it shall not be quiet in our little home in Tite Street for long. I delight to tell you that our notable twosome will soon be added to.

Was ever a woman so blessed as I?

Yours ever with much love and affection,

Constance

*

Dear Otho,

Forgive me not writing sooner. Were you to see me in this very moment, you might see that I have my hands rather full.

I trust you got Oscar's letter, telling you about our little prince. Oscar has barely left my side since he was born, except to write to all his unmarried friends, telling them to remedy the situation immediately. Have a family. We are calling him Cyril. He's so complete.

Fatherhood seems to have prompted Oscar to take himself more seriously, and he is now looking into what he terms 'real and gainful employment', though whether Oscar knows exactly what real and gainful employment might be is a mystery all of its own. You shall be mortified, I know, but *I am thinking of becoming a correspondent to some paper, or else going on the stage: que pensez vous? I want to make some money: perhaps a novel would be better.* [32] Cyril has changed me.

As much as I am grateful to Oscar for safeguarding us, I no longer believe it to be his calling alone. If women are to be taken seriously henceforth, we must be seen to be as hardworking, as dedicated, as committed as our male counterparts, babe in arms or no. One hopes that if other women look to one and sees women such as myself taking up causes, if only for betterment of oneself beyond marriage and motherhood, then surely, I will have done my part. There is so much more that can be done. Oscar understands and supports this, for which I am so grateful. Perhaps it is why God sent him to me.

Our friend... Mr. Heron Allen, however. Oscar asked him to cast Cyril's horoscope, but... the results were somewhat disconcerting, to say the least. He said that Cyril would know great hardship in his life – that it would none of it be easy for him. When we pressed for predictions on future career, his own marriage, for example, Mr. HA became strangely vague. We have, of course, tried to put it from our minds. I don't even know why I mention it here!

We are hoping we shall have a daughter next. We will call her Isola, after Oscar's sister. She died in childhood years ago, but Oscar talks about her often.

Just a note to let you know how we fare. How are you?

All our love,

Constance

*

Dear Otho,

It seems that my every letter must begin with an apology for not being able to write more to you recently. I have been greatly, greatly busy recently, hence my silence. There are two other tiny mouths to feed in this household, not just the one. My debut in Helen of Troy here in London seems to have been rather well-received, but I doubt now that I am the mother again I will have much occasion to tread the boards, sadly. We are all quite well, Oscar, and myself. Cyril grows well. And then, there is Vyvyan. Vyvyan is...

Is it so very awful to confess that things seem so very different with this boy than with his brother? Cyril is healthy, bonnie, happy, our first joy and this child is sickly and... not the daughter we had hoped for. It is quite awful, but we only remembered to register the little thing's birth the other day and when we came to it, to our horror, we realised we neither of us could remember the date. Oscar declared it was the 5th whereas I said it could not have been later than the 2nd. We eventually were able to settle on the 3rd, and it says so on his birth certificate.

Oscar is spending a little more time at his club than at home just now. It gives him the opportunity to work on his writing. Crying children cannot help, of course. Though I do miss him when he is not here. Of course, he has his friends about him, but one cannot deny him that!

Oscar had yesterday such a beautiful letter from the brother of a young man who has died lately in Australia. Beautiful to me I mean because it is so full of this boy's love for Oscar. I will write a copy of it and send it to you. I should like you to see how good O's influence is on young men. [33]

We have a young Canadian gentleman staying with us just now. His name is Robbie Ross. Quite the young gentleman and brother of our friend Alec. He and Oscar are already firm friends.

Oh, Otho, if only there were a way to tell you… Things have been somewhat… difficult between Oscar and myself in certain ways since Vyvyan was born. I feel so tired, so listless since then. Oscar sees and feels it, I know, though he never complains … He is still so sweet to me, but… there is a distance from him that I wish I knew a remedy for… I spent the entirety of my time with Vyvyan feeling larger than an elephant and not wanting to do anything. Perhaps Oscar thought that it would always be that way, and that is why…

There was an incident some time ago that seems to have impressed upon Oscar greatly. I went shopping at Swan and Edgar's and Oscar waited for me outside. As he did, this little creature with hard eyes stopped before him and gave a sort of laugh at him, then simply disappeared back into the crowd. Trivial, you may think, but Oscar said that in that moment, he felt as if an icy cold hand had clutched at his heart and since then, he cannot help but feel a presentiment of some kind of doom. It has not put me at my ease.

I need to give myself things to do, or I shall run mad!

Yours as ever,

Constance

*

Dear Otho,

Simply so much to tell you, I do not know where to start!

I would have written earlier, but I had gatherings at our house in Tite Street. I am having two gatherings a month at present – the first and third Thursday of each month. Yesterday, we hosted Sarah Bernhardt, John Ruskin, Ellen Terry, Lillie Langtry, Henry Irving, Robert Browning, and that funny American man – what is his name? Ah yes - Mr. Mark Twain! Very droll. Our neighbours do get tired that the carriages bringing our guests here take up the road, but I believe I have allayed them for now. I have an autograph book now that is very nearly already full. My parties have even been written about in the Lady's Pictorial! Mother has even deigned come to some of my At Homes. I don't fool myself to think she might have, had I married anyone other than Oscar, and been unable to provide her the company she loves to flatter herself with in my house.

I have been political lately. It has become the fashion to have political parties in London and some of the swells manage to get Gladstone, so I have seen a good deal of him lately and have heard him speak, too, which was a real treat. [34] But it has rather inspired me, and I have been working very closely on something rather dear to my heart, that I know you may not well approve of greatly. But do not be so very surprised if you see in the papers rather soon that my friend Lady Sandhurst has become the first female Member of Parliament! I have been doing all I might to see this happen, and think we are quite close to a victory now!!

What serves to make me somewhat nervous at present, is I am due to speak and open the meeting for the Rational Dress Society. I will have women know that they need not wear corsets and narrow-toed boots in order to be accepted in society, but I myself can't bear the thought of speaking and being listened to by so many women, most of whom I've never met before in my life… Oscar has assured me I will do well, but he will not know, for men are not to be admitted!

Baby is quite strong and fat and long, and he can walk and is beginning to talk. Cyril adores and Vyvyan more or less dislikes me and adores his father but I suppose that will come right in the end. People say he is pretty, but he was prettier when he was waxy and white and delicate. He is not as tall as Cyril was but is very much fatter. [35] Oscar dotes on them both, as they on him.

Is there a chance in your coming to England any time soon, darling? It would be so nice to see you, and to have you meet the boys. Do write me back a note soon, won't you?

Yours with love,

Constance

*

Dear Otho,

I write this letter in anticipation of one from you. Yes, it is indeed true, I am occasionally seen out in public without the chaperone, or indeed presence, of my husband. In fact, it is also true that I am seen in the company of other women, none of us with a male escort to be seen! Not only that but, yes, you have heard it a-right, I occasionally partake in the predominantly male pastime of smoking in public when in said company. Knowing that you will not approve, I have sent this letter to let you know it matters not so much to me that you do not, and therefore, from here, let us say no more about it!

I'm writing chiefly for the newspaper clipping I have included here for you, describing Oscar and myself as 'a literary couple.' Have you yet received your copy of my children's story? 'Was It A Dream'? I can now tell you it is to be published in The Bairn's Annual! Oscar is, of course, beaming with pride - my first published work - and he insists on telling everyone. But next… I think I shall write more. A collection of tales, perhaps. For children. 'There Was Once', by Constance Mary Wilde. Yes, something that Cyril will read one day. And Vyvyan, of course.

This is, of course, if I am able to find the time! When I am not running around after the boys, it seems I am writing Oscar's work for him! That is, he dictates and I write, as neatly as I am able. It is a wonder anyone has read his work at all, for his terrible handwriting, and I am happy to be useful. Oscar jested some time ago that I now am so well acquainted with his work, I should be able to write under his name myself, and not even the publisher would know the difference. I do think that I will tell Oscar again the story I thought of the other day, see if he likes it still on reflection, about a giant in a garden.

And then of course, there is Oscar's Real and Gainful Employment at last, that I am delighted we are to be working on together: 'The Lady's World: A Magazine of Fashion and Society'. We have already decided upon several changes, such as from Lady's World to Women's World, to make it seem more accessible to those who fear that they deserve not the moniker of 'lady'. I helped Oscar write his own letter of application, emphasising that what is not needed is yet another magazine wherein we are lectured on the finer points of millinery, but that we feel we have a voice that speaks in accordance with that which we would use ourselves when speaking with each other in our own parlours. I cannot take credit for the wonderful phrase he used, which I feel must have decided them: *'At present it is too feminine and not sufficiently womanly.'* [36]

Things are rather improved between myself and Oscar quite recently. We consult each other almost daily via letters. He is away from home a little more than I would like, in honesty, but his work needs his attention. There are still certain problems between he and I, but then one would be a fool not to expect any in a marriage. I still do believe we have made a fine match. I am still very much in love with him.

I have been for years thinking about this terrible passion of jealousy, and I am quite certain that the only way to conquer it is to love more intensely. Love will swallow up even the pangs of jealousy. Surely if one is jealous of one's husband it is because one thinks it is possible to make him love one more, and the only way to do that is to love him more, and make him feel that no one else loves him as much. [37]

Do write to me soon, won't you, Otho? If I forget to return, you can see why, but I am anxious to hear all your news.

All my love.

Constance

*

Dear Otho,

I am not in the best of humours as I write to you.

Not only has it been ruled that Mrs. Sandhurst gained her seat in Parliament illegally, but the whole thing has been grossly satirized by the tabloid newspapers. And in Punch magazine there have not only been articles but cartoons...

Oh, I am not well. I took a trip to Brighton to see Mama some while ago, but you will have no doubt heard by now that Mr. SK has taken to living in Hastings, very happily without her. This has done nothing for her temperament; she is still all icy cold. My holiday was not restful, I daresay, and therefore I'm returned much earlier than I thought I would and, because of this, I am still ill. Oscar, on occasion, will take me out to the theatre to pick me up from my melancholia, when he has the time to spare, of course.

Just now, the boys have whooping cough, and I am up and down all night tending to them. Every time I am ill, however, it seems to be my back that hurts me the most, and nothing ever remedies it. Even when the rest of me is ill, the pain there seems to stubbornly remain.

I have just been reading Mr. Leo Tolstoy's 'Work While We Have The Light' and feel more depressed than ever. I am more certain than ever that I am leading an absolutely useless life and yet don't see how to alter it. [38]

I am getting more & more convinced that my nurse is not very wise. [39] *My nurse has taken it into her head to be married this July which is to say the least of it, annoying.* [40] *She is so angry at my sending Vyvyan away from her... I love him as much as I do Cyril, but he is not interesting yet because his soul has not awaked.* [41]

I cannot make out whether it is my fault or Oscar's that he is so cold to me and so nice to others. He is gone to Birmingham to see his play acted there tonight. His butler knows his other plans and I know nothing. Darling, what am I to do? [42]

He writes to me every day while he is working, but there is such distance between the two of us now, that I don't know what to do to remedy it. At least he has his friends around him, especially his greatest friend, Lord Alfred, who I believe Oscar has a name for - Bosie, or something like, he calls him. He's a lovely young man, provides Oscar with great company, I am sure, but he does dog Oscar somewhat. Even when we were on holiday this year, Lord Alfred joined us. Then, just as it was time to leave and come home again, he fell rather ill, and Oscar stayed behind to tend him... in his sickness....

The last time I came back to London, I arrived at Victoria station, and waited for Oscar to collect me, but he arrived. I assumed he must be busy, or it had slipped his mind. When I arrived at Tite Street, there was a mountain of post behind the door; it was as if no one had been there at all for weeks! I gathered some and took what seemed to be the most important to the Savoy, where Oscar is staying and asked him if he would come home soon, as when the boys return, they will be asking for him. And he told me...

He told me that he had forgotten our address.

I am in the wrong mood to be writing. Forgive me, dearest. I'll write again soon.

Yours,

Constance

WOMEN OF FORGOTTEN IMPORTANCE

*

Dear Otho,

I write to you in the hope that you will be able to provide some sore-needed advice. It has come to my attention that the boys' education needs to be decided upon with some urgency, and I hoped there might be some good European schools, you with your own fine brood, that you might recommend for boys of my sons' dispositions.

Before you write to me to inform that the boys' education is rather Oscar's realm, this, I am all too aware of it. However, but Oscar is not present enough to be able to see to it, therefore it falls to me. I shall not have my sons attend bad schools. I have read enough papers and heard enough whispers now to understand that everyone expects Oscar's sons to be carbon copies of himself. My sons are half myself as much as they are half of him. I scarce get a moment where I cannot find myself worrying about Vyvyan. I send him here and there for other care, and Cyril is so annoyed at me for parting them, but what can I do? And I will not have this over familiarity; I will not have this over femininity that Oscar -

Oh god, Otho… I feel as if I have sinned, and yet everything is in my mind. I have committed nothing at all. Is it possible to commit a sin in one's mind alone and still be clean? I have… met someone. His name is Arthur Humphreys. Oh god, I should not admit it to you! As I have said, nothing in the world has happened between us. Nothing but words. Words that my husband once said to me… I have merely gotten carried away and I am determined that it shall go no further, but I have written to him. We talked. I miss that most of all. Talking and debating and discussing with another equal to one's own intellect. I couldn't help it… I missed him so.

I knew, however, that the entire charade had to come to an end when I came across a manuscript of Oscar's latest attempt. It is a shameful parody of our lives. The hero of the piece, if one can call him that, enlists his wife to flirt with another man for his own gain, but, finding that they have fallen in love, the hero, if one can call him such, takes his own life… I am resolved to never speak to Mr. Humphreys again.

There is another matter, one I shame to write. It may well have come to your attention by this point, Otho, that myself and my husband have been leading increasingly separated lives, and I might spend my every moment wondering why. Yet, some while ago, Oscar came to me very much his old self again, attentive and cheerful to see me. I was so pleased that it seemed we might return to our old ways, that when Oscar proposed that he had need of my help for some research he was undertaking, I was only too happy to oblige, without asking what it might entail. It appears my husband had become increasingly interested in Spirituality, more specifically, with one particular group - The Order of the Golden Dawn. He told me he had reached a point in his studies of them that the next stage was definitely to become a member to gain more knowledge, but he, with his reputation such as it is, would surely be looked on by the Order with great suspicion. However, he reasoned, my reputation is quite as his.

Otho, the things that I learned as I was made to study to join their ranks. The things I read and found out about. The people I met whose names I dare not write here. The things I was made to swear! That on pain of being struck mute, paralysed, even to be done to death, if any of what I was privy to was discussed without the Order. And then I, for its main purpose, detailed as much, and answered as many of Oscar questions as he put forth to me, without thought. It was for my husband's work! All I wanted for him to see me again, but I begin for reasons that even I cannot adequately put into words, to believe, I should not have done that...

Things have indeed begun to improve between myself and Oscar rather recently. I receive almost daily letters from him now, and he visits much more frequently these past few weeks. It is quite marked, his difference in behaviour. I do not like to pry too deeply into Oscar's personal affairs, but I cannot help but think it is perhaps something to do with Lord Alfred, with Bosie. They have been very great friends for a long while now. Lord Alfred's father is apparently something of a tyrant of a man - The Marquess of Queensbury - so naturally, a sensitive young man would look to the likes of Oscar for paternal feeling, but it would seem that he has been running Oscar quite ragged. Trips abroad at the drop of a hat, dinner with champagne most evening, gifts! And you know what Oscar is – never satisfied unless everyone is happy and amused, only too happy to oblige. Well, this is why I believe there to be some connection, because Oscar's change in behaviour has coincided with his resolve not to see Lord Alfred again. He has seemingly not spoken to him or even of him in nigh on a fortnight. I cannot think what must have passed between them.

It is so very difficult though, and puts me in such a position. You see, I received a letter from Lord Alfred only this morning. He asked me to use any power I have over my husband to entreat Oscar to see him again, for he misses him so! He wrote so sadly, I felt in that moment as if someone understood me quite keenly. That he knew almost as much as I what it is to have Oscar and yet to not have Oscar… Perhaps, if I do speak to Oscar, I can encourage some kind of reconciliation. Perhaps some friendship can be salvaged from it?

Otho, I read back this letter and ask that you do get rid of this letter immediately. Sometimes I must write to confess and then I cannot bear to have a single piece of the memory I have attached to the writing left to me, or even in the world at all.

Yours,

Constance.

*

Dear Otho,

I am writing against my better judgement, and I have delayed in writing for the greatest length of time, but indeed it will no longer do. I must ask you. When you left Nellie, your first wife… Was there anything that she did that made you… not love her anymore? Especially after the birth of the children? What changed for you after that?

The truth is, Otho, I am quite out of my mind with worry these days. I have not seen Oscar now for two months. He writes but, of course it is not the same. I worry sometimes that people think there is something greatly wrong with our marriage. I cannot think what to say or do. Once upon a time, it was my face that accompanied Oscar in the parodies, and I knew we would always be the subject of ridicule for some. But now, instead, I open a newspaper and find Bosie's face next to my husband's instead and the most ridiculous things suggested.

Only the other day, I was out with friends, when one of them, seeing the others' attention diverted, grabbed me firmly by the wrist and insisted: 'Isn't it time you got Oscar in hand, Constance?' When I asked her what on earth she meant, and the other ladies' attention brought back, she paled, and pretended that not a thing had happened. I have thought of writing to her, but doubt I should get a response. I do not understand! What is it that is happening that everyone besides myself seems to know, and yet no one will speak to me of? I am quite certain now, as I have never been, that there is not another woman in his life, but if not that, then what!

There must have been something I did to make him so distant. Despite his detachment, my husband is not a morally unsound person. Why have his affections change? How does one go about changing them back again?

The horrible thing is that I miss him. Cyril and Vyvyan are close of an age to be too much for me on occasion. He could send me back a little more money than he does, as it begins to seem that if things continue in this fashion, by the end of the year, I shall have to let the staff go, and then where shall I be? With so much to do by myself! On top of all this, I am in absolute agony with my back once more, and there are days when it is painful even to stand.

I was thinking of Oscar tonight in fact, wondering if there was something I could say or do to make him see me again, to make me seem charming and entertaining as the company he seems to love dearer than me now, when I was brought his note.

'Dear Constance… I am coming to see you at nine o'clock. Please be in – it is important. Ever yours, Oscar.' [43]

Brief and vague. That is not Oscar's style. Oh Otho. I have in this moment the presentiment of some terrible, terrible danger on the horizon for all of us. What can any of it mean?

Constance

*

Dear Otho,

I am at Tite Street just for the night. You can write to me at my usual address in Genoa, as I return in the morning. I thought that while I was in England, I ought to look in and see if there was anything that might be salvaged before the house was sold for good. But it would seem that Oscar's debtors arrived long before I did. Only the meagerest of my possessions is now left to me.

It is very strange to be returned here now. It is so silent. I cannot remember this house every being silent. I remember when it rang with our laughter and love. My tiny sons… my loving husband… Our guests, the great and the good. Politicians, writers, artists, thinkers…

My last operation gave me some relief, you'll be glad to hear. But Dr. Bossi seems to believe that there needs to be another. I am so tired, I don't know that I shall live through it, but the alternative is simply to continue to waste away as I have been doing for the past few years. Not the best of options, but at least I am aware of them. *I am tired of doctors and no doctor finding out what to do with me... I am lamer than ever and have almost given up hope of ever getting well again.* [44]

Do you know, it occurs to me I might have not been here since the trial. That of the Marquess of Queensbury. Oscar visited me late one evening to tell me what The Marquess had done, and that he could see nothing but a libel suit in it. I told him to drop it. I told him it didn't matter what the Marquess had said or done, but rather than ignorance, it were the challenging of such remarks and insinuations that something told me might be the ruin of us all. When he left here that evening, he seemed to have listened to me and accepted good counsel, to be resolved.

But then, Bosie had his say. Had to have his own way. Then the suit fell through and Oscar was arrested. I can still remember the actors from his play, in sight of he that gave them the work that meant they did not starve, and they denounced him, told all these...stories! Then the theatres removed his name from the billing. Removed his name? Oscar Wilde's name? And then, what could I do but follow suit?

It is strange how everyone always feels they must take a stance, a side in matters such as this. There have been those who were kind, as kind as they could be given the circumstances. There have been many who have been unable to associate with us in any way since. Of course, there have also been the brutes, who came about as soon as they could smell the scandal in the air, prying for every penny that might be available.

I feel the pity from others. The belittling. Once upon a time, I had been my own person. Oscar had always eclipsed me and I had never worried about it. But once, I had a name all my own – I was Constance. Now, I'm simply 'Wilde's Wife'. That is the kindest thing they call me. They must think I cannot hear them. That I cannot read the papers. 'It's Wilde's wife I feel sorry for. Can you imagine being her, just now?' Ten, even five years ago, they'd have crawled over broken glass to be me. Now I'm simply a distorted shadow of Oscar. Suddenly I am no longer a real person at all. Simply 'Wilde's Wife'.

Yet it is all my fault! Bosie blames me, have you heard? It was my fault. I made Oscar unhappy.

'If she had treated him properly and stuck to him...as a really good wife would have done, he would have gone on loving her to the end of his life. Obviously, she suffered a good deal

and deserves sympathy, but she fell woefully short of the height to which she might have risen.' [45]

Otho, I am not very well…

I saw him today. Oscar. No colourful coats, no carnations. His hair clipped and his skin – he barely looked himself. He's suited to letters and parties and the most energy he expended was staying up all night, but what they have him doing in that god-forsaken place… He looks ill. I sat opposite him and told him what I had come all this way to tell him.

'Your mother's died, Oscar,' I told him. 'I am so very sorry.'

When his grief had subsided a little, he asked me where I was staying. I told him I was abroad, in Genoa in Italy. He expressed surprise, asked me what had made me come so far to deliver the news of his mother personally, especially with my ill health. And I couldn't tell him. I said, of course, that I hadn't wanted him to discover such things from unfriendly or indifferent lips. I asked him how his ear was treating him, you know he fell and injured it recently, and he answered 'It plagues me, as your back does you.'

We have been married almost twelve years, and now, we talk of nothing with each other.

To my surprise, however, suddenly he lifted his head and said to me: 'I suppose you want a divorce,' he said. 'I'll not deny you one, should you ask it of me.'

I told him he did not know what the three of us had suffered by his hand. I told him I had had to change the children's names, and mine, to spare us all the disgrace. I told him of the humiliation and the journalists, the looks and whispers I detected even for the few hours I had been in England. I told him of the friends I had never heard from since the scandal broke, and of my own awful financial straits he had left us in without a thought. I told him of the daily pain I lived with, physical now coupled with emotional, the minute I woke up each morning. I told him he did not *know* what we had suffered, and that I wouldn't divorce him, because even after everything all of us had been through, and what everyone seemed to not have realised somewhere along the journey, was that the shame and the torment and the measures taken to keep the rocked boat of our lives afloat seemed little to being told and realising that the man you love…

II told him he had to give up his parental rights to them. It was for the best. He hated that as well, but I told him it was for their benefit, and whereas he had failed to look after us, I could not fail them. I haven't been the best of mothers, I know it, but I did my best given the extraordinary circumstances, and eventually, he agreed.

And even as I left Reading Gaol, these scraps of hope were about my heart. He'd been mine first. Maybe someday...

I finally have the boys settled in their respective schools, after their expulsion from the last two. I left it too late to school them, I think, which I regret. However, Cyril wrote to me from his school in Germany quite recently, eager to tell me he is keen to be a military officer when he is grown. All I could think was that there were no real wars just now, nothing that could put my boy in any real danger. We've probably come too far to have such an horrendous war, so I shan't discourage him. I'm sure he will make a fine officer.

I saw Vyvyan in Monaco in February while on holiday from his Jesuit school. He seems *very happy, as clever as he can be, very sure of himself as always, and mad about stamps. He is also mad about coins.* [46] How shall I ever not blame him for what I know he did not do intentionally? It was simply that as soon as he was with us... Oscar just drifted away. No one could control Oscar, though. Not even Oscar. Especially not Oscar. Yet my life has had moments of great joy. Frustratingly enough, most of the good parts I seem to owe, directly or in part, to him.

You shall probably think it grossly morbid, Otho, but I have been thinking rather deeply recently on my legacy. How I shall be remembered once I am gone. A fine thing to think, one might say, considering I'm not yet forty. I thought the other day how nice it would be to be remembered as a woman who fought for the rights of other women. There is still much of a way to go, but we have made a definite start. Then I thought, perhaps it might be just as nice to be remembered as a woman of letters - for my literary works, I mean. I hope that my works, meagre and few as they are, will be read and enjoyed for many years to come. I caught myself at the last thinking how nice it should be if I were simply remembered as the mother of two wonderful children. They are, after all, my greatest work.

However, a dull fear comes upon me, Otho. The fear that, if I am to be remembered at all, it shall probably be as nothing more than Mrs. Oscar Wilde.

Otho. When you get this letter, will you come and see me in Genoa immediately? Please? Drop everything and come at once. I am not quite sure how I can say it, Otho, but, you see… I am… not… well…

The Pendle Witch

Introduction

In contrast to *The Witch In The Woods* and *Mrs. Oscar Wilde*, there is no particular story or circumstance surrounding how I came to pen *The Pendle Witch*. It was rather a bizarre gut feeling - an instinct to learn more and do something about the story that came in waves, and a decision that I wanted to write another play at that particular time.

I originally saw a documentary about the original Witches of Pendle, or The Lancaster Witches - *The Pendle Witch Child,* presented by the poet Simon Armitage, who I'd seen at the theatre in Sheffield as a schoolgirl. The strange thing was that I originally went looking for the programme, or some other information on the Pendle Witches, and I can't remember how, or when, I first heard of them to spark my interest. If I were any more superstitious, I'd probably be tempted to believe that somehow, Jennet, the character whose perspective *TPW* is told from, was making sure in whatever preternatural method was at her disposal, that someone hungry for stories of women from history knew that hers was one that had not yet fully been told. In fact, even with the level of superstition I'm currently at, you'd probably find it a far easier time convincing me it was that, than it wasn't.

Sensationalist, and surprisingly taking place almost a century before the Salem Witch Trials, the true story of the Witches of Pendle sounds almost contrived itself. In August of 1612, ten people were put on trial for witchcraft at the Lancashire Assizes, three of them from the same family - the Devices (possibly a variation of the name Davies / Davis). The youngest of this family, the only one not accused, was a little girl, supposedly only nine years old at the time (in fact she must have been at least eleven, possibly nearly twelve). This girl, Jennet Device, testified in court against the rest of her family, specifically her mother and brother, denouncing them as witches, with the apparent presence and capability of a seasoned speaker. The clerk to the court, Thomas Potts, mentions in his book, *The Wonderfull Discoverie of Witches In The Countie of Lancaster*, with how much confidence and poise Jennet delivered her statements.

As a result, her mother, brother and sister - her entire immediate family - were sent straight to the gallows, along with the seven other people from the local district, for the crime of causing death or harm by witchcraft. Horrific, indeed, are the bare bones of this unfortunate story of betrayal and communal superstition, but I felt that a vital point had been made missed in all the source material I was able to find.

At the very centre of this tragic tale, there was a little girl.

I remembered myself at eleven: clever and inquisitive, but scatty and quick-to-act before thinking. Yet I also remember how easy it was to influence me. Children are very easy to manipulate; easy to frighten. Tell a child that an evil force will come and claim them if they do not obey you, and with gentle reinforcement, they will do anything you say. The things attested by Jennet Device against her mother and brother not only sound implausible to the modern ear, but they make no sense when one considers that she was eliminating all her carers and close friends in this world. Why would a child do such a thing to her family members, were it not true, as we can assume her outlandish testimony (including imps that take the form of dogs causing the deaths of neighbours and acquaintances) to be?

Unless, of course, there was some very calculated manipulation involved on behalf of those who stood to gain reputation at such a scandalous trial. Unless there was a magistrate who meant to make his name under a king who was both superstitious and greatly interested in witches. Unless the juvenile Jennet, not so much gave testimony on the 18th of August 1612, but rather took to the stage, and delivered lines that she had meticulously learnt, under careful tutelage of one who believed he would gain much from a Guilty verdict?

I went looking for the story of Jennet Device in its entirety. I had a somewhat workable picture of what had happened prior to the trial, the circumstance she had been in, and even ideas of why she might have worked with Justice of the Peace Roger Nowell, but after the trial itself - nothing. From becoming an overnight sensation in the courtroom and receiving such praise, she promptly disappears back into obscurity. I had forgotten that she was yet another person of no specific importance beyond what Nowell, a wealthy and influential man on a quest, had been able to get out of her during a time of widespread paranoia and deeply-rooted superstition. There were not the equivalents of magazines and tabloids of the time that might follow the now-infamous Jennet into the next phase of her life.

The only other mention of her after that - and even then, it is not certain if it is really the same person or simply someone who happens to have the same name - is two decades later: a Jennet Device from the Pendle area was herself incarcerated in Lancaster Castle and, amazingly, accused of causing death or harm by witchcraft, the very same thing for which her family hanged. She was accused of having a hand in the death of a woman called Isabel, wife to a man called William Nutter, a possibly distant cousin to Alice Nutter, one who was hanged in the same trial that claimed Jennet's family. When the trial fell apart and her accusers themselves were arrested, Jennet was acquitted, but is still on public record as having been in the prison several years later. That is the last glimmer of insight as to what became of the Pendle Witch Child.

While some may think of this as karma served and justice done, I feared that it might not be so straightforward as this. There was a very real possibility that in fact, Jennet was a name one could put to yet another female who had slipped through the cracks and had been failed grossly by the system in place. It was with this sad likelihood that I began writing what might have been her story.

No one knows what happened in the interim years; no one knows why she said what she originally said against her family for sure, in a time when her testimony was only allowed because accepting the claims of children was advocated by the nervy Gunpowder Plot king, James I, in his book *Daemonologie*. We know no more about the twists of fate which meant she ended up labelled a Witch herself as a grown woman, in a time when the Queen of Bohemia advocated burning them rather than hanging. Most sadly for myself as a writer of her story from her perspective, no one knows how it ultimately ended for her, or where she is buried. The sad likelihood is that, unable to pay back for her time in prison, as was the way in Medieval Britain, she remained in Lancaster Castle in the Witches' Tower until she eventually died.

The prospects of any kind of happy ending for her are unbearably bleak, and I fear she rests in an unmarked pauper's grave somewhere near the grounds of the Castle, likely with many other victims of the harsh conditions of a 17th Century prison. Even worse, is that with so flimsy information to go on, there is no way to find her now. Given all this, I took it upon myself to fill in the gaps that record had left me, and create a fictionalised monologue around the very real events, painting a portrait of a woman who, when one stands back and looks at the picture as a whole, may have been far more victim than she ever was villain.

A couple of people believe that I have been mistaken, and mean to call the play 'The Pendle Witches', but this is a story told, as usual, from the perspective of one person, reflecting on the events leading up to and following the trial she was a part of, which while was not the first of its kind, it was quite literally law-changing. The trial is still spoken of, and popular, for both tourists and historians, four hundred years after it took place.

LEXI WOLFE

The Pendle Witch

Nethen, before yer gets too settled, let's be clear about some things, shall us? This part o' the cell is mine. I stick to mine and don't come to your parts. That there is yours. You stay to yours, I'll stay to mine, and we won't have any problems. You'll not be able to sneak up on me, so don't try it. Besides, yer try anything, you'll end up like the others. I'd ask yer what yer all in for, but I don't care. Some o' yer won't be 'ere the week. Some'll get dragged out to the gallows, and it's nowt to do wi' me. And some'll go the way o' the others, what were in 'ere before yer. Tha gets it when tha's in places like this, all crammed in together, the way us are. Tha'll cough, not be able to breathe, feel warm to the touch, but feel cold as ice inside. Then tha'll start to see things wha' others cannot, and that's when tha knows - Death has come for thee. Maybe it's that what makes 'em reckon it's me what does away wi' em. Nowt to do wi' me. They just reckon, wi' my past it must be me what makes 'em die, but if yer don't wrong me, it's nowt to do wi' me.

You don't know who I am, d'yer? They're 'avin a laugh nah, putting yer in wi' a woman they still reckon might still be a witch and don't even tell yer. And before yer go scramblin' for the door, they're used to people askin' to lerrem out, they never do. And anyway, like I say, don't meddle wi' me, I won't meddle wi' none o' you.

Did they not even tell yer yer were comin' to Witches Tower? That's what they call this place, this part o' Lancaster Castle. 'As been for years. It's not named cuz o' me, neither. It's named for me mam, and me granny. All o'em. Ten o'em.

Isabel Robey, Katherine Hewitt, Jane Bulcock, her son John. Alice Nutter. Anne Whittle. Anne Redferne. Elizabeth Device, James Device, Alison Device.

I know their names. 'Course I do. Couldn't ever forget 'em, could I?

And now I've said that, you'll start to think to theesen. Late at night, in yer own part o' the cell, or maybe in a day or two, you'll start thinking on what

I've said, and yer'll come to me and say "Hi! I reckon I know who tha is - tha must be Jennet Device! Youngest o' them witches, int tha? That's who tha is!"

Then yer'll want to know. You'll want to know about the girl who said all my family were witches. What saw 'em swing from the gallows a morn not so lang after. Then yer'll each want to know how I come to be 'ere, called the same as them. You'll want to know, so I might as well tell thee. All of yer.

These important people. They make yer think they've all this power, like the Almighty Himself, but they only care if tha've done something wrong, or if tha's a threat to em. Ten years or more, they never helped us. Not until they feared us…

*

There were five o' us, livin' in me grandmother's house when I were young. Eldest were me Granny, who others near and far called Old Demdike; then there were Squintin' Lizzie, who were 'er daughter and my mother, called Elizabeth Device; eldest o' us were my brother James, and then me sister Alizon. And last of all, me - Jennet.

They said that we were from Pendle, but we weren't, not really. Pendle Hill were just nearest place they knew. Everyone knows Pendle Hill. We lived, in fact, on the edge of Pendle Forest. They liked to make fun of us, them what lived further into the villages and the towns, them what went to church and lived close to one another. House were only just big enough to fit us in, but they called it Malkin Tower. Do you not know the word? Malkin round our way means 'whore' or 'slut'. They don't know nothing, though. I were baptized at Newchurch in 1600. I know cuz it were same year me father died, and they all hated me for it. Well, me mam and James did.

"Don't mind 'er," me brother James would say. "She's just a little bastard."

"I'm not!" I'd cry back. "You're a bastard."

Then he'd lam me, and say he was not, that he'd not caused our dad to die. I asked me mam what he meant from time to time, but she thumped me too, so I never asked more in the end. I didn't know anythin' about it until final, Alizon told me:

"It's not tha fault. There's a witch. She lives on t'other side o' the Hill. They call her Old Chattox. She's seen men dead for slights on her. When us first came 'ere, she thought Granny, bein' a cunning woman, made people come to us instead of 'er, so 'er lot broke in and stole all we 'ad. Dad were so afraid o' 'er, he used to pay her 8 pounds of oatmeal a year, just for 'er to leave us alone. Paid it regular, every year - no trouble. Then, it were the year tha were born, he couldn't quite get enough together, so he didn't pay 'er. When he were dyin', 'e said it was 'er what cursed him. It weren't thee, Jennet. It were the witch."

I liked Alizon better than James, as she were kinder to me. She missed me brother Henry, what were born five years before me, but died year before I were born, so I never knew 'im. But best I liked of all was Granny. Wi' dad gone, there was only askin' others for what they could spare for us to do, beside me Granny. She may have been old and near blind, but nobody messed wi' 'er. They'd come around for Old Demdike when they had need of her, they would. She were really old, and, even when I were little, and she couldn't see reight well, but she were always kind to me, teaching me what she was doin' and shieldin' me when James wanted to get at me. When I'd sit close by her, she'd teach me some of the things she'd be doin', and what for, and sometimes she'd send me out to fetch for 'er. I had to be really careful what I brought back for her, when she was making things, 'cuz if I got it wrong, then the whole thing she were tryin' to make might be ruined.

One time I did bring back the wrong thing. She'd needed this yellow flower, so she said, but what she truly needed were dandelions. But she were confused, as it were the wrong time o' year for 'em, and I were still only little, so I brought back daffodils. When she realised, and told me I'd done wrong, me mam and James, and even Alizon, they laughed, like, why would I get it so wrong to not know this flower, and bring daffodils instead? I remember goin' bright red. But me Gran pulled me close, and she whispered to me:

"I'll tell thee a secret, Jennet Device, that even thy mother, who's been wi' me and watchin' me, not as close as she should've, for more'n forty years by my reckonin', even she does not know it. It's not always the right plant or the moonlight that you need to work your charms and drinks. If it were so easy, they wouldn't try and make us out to be somethin' unnatural. Sometimes, the greatest of findings come when pure chance has brought thee somethin' instead of another. That is how we learn and find anew. Besides, I reckon tha could right now make me a thing I asked thee to better than thy mother could. Don't be afeared to find out for theesen."

There was somethin' wrong wi' me brother James. We all knew it, but if we said anythin', then he'd get angry. He was littler than 'e should've been, and 'e'd lose his temper so fast, and could be so rude, that when I were still really young, me mam stopped him from goin' out to beg. She said she 'ad more problems from him doin' so than less, and people'd not come to see Granny if they feared walkin' into 'im, if 'e carried on. I don't know what it were. Alizon said he's always been like it, but that he'd got worse as he go' older. This one time, I came back with Alizon from the village, and we'd had a good day. People'd given and we knew we'd be able to get by a bit. James were sittin', waitin' for us, on a rock by the house, in a foul temper.

"You're late," says he. "Mam's needin' yer for help within."

"Why didn't tha do it?" Alizon asks.

"Dad never did," he says wi' a huff. "Dunt see why I shall 'av ter."

"That's a shame," says Alizon, laughin'. "Now tha's got no use at all!"

As the words passed her lips, we both knew it should not have been said. 'Is face were like the colour of autumn leaves, and he takes off running after us, both o' us screamin' as we go. I hear the door thump open behind us, and me mam comes out the house and shouts at him to leave us, but he dunt listen. I were the smallest and couldn't run fast as Alizon, and I tripped and I fell, and so he caught me - he's over me. He picks me up and throws me back against the ground, smacks me across the face, whacks me back the other side, me ears ringing like the church bell on Sunday. I can 'ear Mam shoutin' after us, but she can't run fast as James. He takes me by the shoulders, throwin' me back against the ground till I thought my head'd cave in.

By the time Mam's caught him up, my lip and my nose are bleedin, and my eye hurts to open. Every part of my face stings. Takes 'er another few moments to get 'im off, and I almost thought he'd turn on 'er. Alizon's a little way away from fear, as Mam shoves James back towards the house, tellin' 'im to leave me, for I'm only little. Then she turns on me: "And tha, little devil, stop angerin' 'im." And us all went home. Took me far longer to climb up the last part o' that little hill than it had the first time. Alizon stayed as if to help me, but Mam shouted at her, and she went on without me.

It weren't the first or the last time, but it hurt the most. I got more money dropped in ma hand those two weeks followin' than I ever 'ad before, lookin' the way I did. I musta been - seven or eight?

It's strange how when tha looks back, tha realises it were all so long ago, feels like another life, and yet it might 'ave happened yesterday for thee. But strange enough, thing I reckon I remember most, were That Night, dead clear. The night when Alizon came home upset, and everything started to go wrong.

She were the last back through the door that night, and she comes in quiet, white in the face. Me mam runs to 'er, asks what had happened - reckon someone's forced themselves on her, but no.

"I swear, mam, I didn't mean it, I didn't mean it," she says, near cryin'. "I just meant to get some pins, that were all. Granny asked me for some pins, the other day, for her work, so I asked for some. From this pedlar, John Law 'is name is, comin' down the lane. I ask 'im, and 'e asks if I've enough for 'em. I told him I couldn't afford em, but just some, for pity's sake, for what little I had on me, I 'ad need of 'em. But he wouldn't open his pack. So I... I..."

She need not say what she'd done. They don't reckon it's just me Granny, not just Old Demdike what's got power. A witch's curse killed me dad. They say it can make a plague come on thee, bring thee bad fortune, or even just make it so when you set to milk churning, the butter won't come, and so, few cross us. It's the one thing 'as to get our own back, to keep folk from crossin' us. So we knew that Alizon had cursed the pedlar that day.

"It weren't a bad curse, and I've never known it work so quick before, no so as I could see it happen before me own eyes! I didn't mean him to fall down. I watch 'im walk a little way, and 'is pack gets too heavy for 'im, and 'e falls t'ground. Can't move none, dunt speak. And all what's about look at him, then see he can't get up none, so they bring him to an inn, lay 'im down in the bed there. I peered in after. He looks so bad, mam, one side of his face askew, can't walk himself, can't form words, can only lift the one arm and not t'other at all! But I swear - I didn't mean it! I didn't mean it so bad, not at all!"

We all look at one another. Me Granny's grinnin' quietly to herself in the corner. Reckon she knew as one o' us was goin' to be a cunning woman to follow after her on day, and all she had to do was wait for it. But Mam paid her no mind.

Mam takes Alizon by the shoulders, tells 'er she's just bein' nesh. This pedlar'll be well again, sure enough, says she. And me mam ought to know. They don't call her Squintin' Lizzie for nothin'. One eye is where is should be in 'er 'ead. The other's much farther down, down 'ere on 'er cheek. I never dared ask 'er who it was cursed her, but she's not suffered for it. Neither will this pedlar for so little a curse, she says as much. Just gives Alizon some broth and tells her to come out o' it, none's goin' o reckon she's had aught to do wi' this man fallin' ill, and it's only her word what says aught's happened, if he can't even speak.

But Alizon's still so upset. I heard her weepin' and tossin', just across the room from me all night.

*

Days go by. By now, all of us 'ave all forgot about thie pedlar and 'is trouble, and we go about our business as is so usual. So, when the door swings inward and a man stands there, lookin' cross and determined, we've no notion at first what he wants.

"Where is she?" he demands, this man. "This girl what's maliciously bewitched my father. Which one of yer did it? Which one of yer were it?"

We condemn Alizon merely by turnin' to look a' 'er. He launches 'imself across the room towards her and grabs 'er by the wrist. "Come wi' me, nar!" he commands. "Come wi' me and put 'im reight. It's a crime, that is, cursin' an old man what's done thee little wrong. Come wi' me nar, and take it from 'im."

This man, this Abraham Law, son of this lamed pedlar, John, 'e holds Alizon's wrist still and starts to drag 'er towards the door. All is panic. None o' us know what to do. Me mam shouts, as she always does, me and Gran starts to feel 'er way along the wall as if to be bar between this man and the door. James, trying to be the man o' the mouse, tries to snatch Alizon back again, but this Abraham Law's easy twice the size o' 'im. So all us can do is watch as Alizon, still cryin', puts up hardly a fight hersen, and just disappears with this man down the road towards the village.

There were nowt to be done right then, so we did nothin', but wait. It were one o' them times where it happened so sudden and unexpected, only a little time later, we might never have believed it 'ad happened at all. Just afore it's truly dark, Alizon comes back through the door, lookin' even more mournful than the other day.

"He's lamed for sure, mam," she says softly. "There were nowt I could do. Only a little better now than when I last saw 'im. Doctor dunt know what to do for 'im neither. 'Im and 'is son, they asked if I could take it off again. I said I were sorry, that I'd take it from 'im and onto mesen if only I knew, if I knew 'ow, but I didn't. And Mr. Law said 'e forgave me all the same.... But what do I know about puttin' someone reight?"

And we settled down once again for the night. But there were a hush in the house, like none o' us dared speak too loud.

Have yer ever been at the edge of a hole, or a well, and tha knows tha's alone, nobody else about thee, but even so, as tha peers down into its depths, tha's certain that there's someone just over tha shoulder, ready as soon as tha drops wariness, to push thee in? It were that kind of feelin' that settled over the 'ouse that evenin', none of us knowin' what were comin' next.

*

Next morn, us were all resolved to forget about this John Law, though we feel sorry for 'is lamin'. We don't expect nothin' from it again. But then, there's a poundin' on the door. None as we know go knockin' on the door. They just come in, usual, no bother wi' knockin', so me mam is wary as she opens the door.

Beyond are two men, dressed much nicer than most what comes round our way. "We seek for one Alizon Device," the one man announces importantly. "Is she within?"

"Why?" me mam asks. "What do you want with 'er? I'm 'er mother."

"The magistrate 'as called for 'er," comes the answer. "Wants to ask 'er about the lamin' of John Law, as attested by his son."

I could tell me mam were about to argue, but Alizon stopped 'er, walkin' past and straight into these men's arms, and off they go. It were so strange. No shoutin' or screamin' or fightin' a' all, nothin' like the other day - one minute she were there, and then she weren't. And if you'd asked me at the time, I'd 'a' probably told you that Alizon would like be back again later that day, just like she were the yesterday. Little were I to know that I'd never behold 'er face a' 'ome again. Little were I to know.

A day passes, then another, and another. Alizon still not returned. Me mam starts to get agitated. Alizon's never been away from home so lang before, and me mam wants to know where she is, who's keepin' 'er, when they sendin' 'er back, are they mistreatin' 'er? For we've been told nothin'. She sends James and I down into the village to ask for any who's seen 'er, but I turn up nothin' - they won't talk to a little child. When we come back, James 'as found all that we know.

"She's still wi' magistrate, I were told," he says. " 'E lives a way away though, mam. Across in a reight big 'ouse called 'Read Hall'. No knowin' when she's comin' 'ome, though."

The next day, me mam reckons it's been lang enough, and she's bent on gettin' hersen to this Read 'All, fetchin' up her brother Christopher to come wi' er, and bring Alizon home again, by force if necessary. But there comes yet another knock at the door.

This man and his partner, same as before, stand beyond, but no Alizon with 'em. "Elizabeth Southerns and Elizabeth Device," says the man what talks. "Mr. Roger Nowell is wanting to see you both."

"See us?" me mam repeats like she doesn't understand. "See us why? And to see me mother as well as me? Wha' on earth for? Dunt tha know she can barely see 'er 'and in front o' 'er face, she's so near blind? Dunt tha knows she 'ardly leaves the 'ouse f'r 'ow old she is? What does this Nowell man want wi' either o' us?"

"Nothin' to do wi' me, Mrs. Device," says this man, bolder than 'e were before. "The magistrate wants to see you both, thee and thy mother, at once, and I'm instructed to bring you to 'im, whether you come willingly, or no."

She didn't shout, but she did argue and make a fuss, and off she went, me Granny on 'er arm, all o' 'em hobblin' slowly down the road, for they can only go so fast as me Gran. James 'ad been out that morn, findin' things o' use to bring back, so when 'e returns, I 'ave to tell 'im what's happened while e's been gone.

"Why didn't tha stop 'em?" he demands of me angrily. "Why didn't tha tell 'em to mind their own and be off?" And 'e pushes me into the wall, then wallops me for good measure. We spoke little to one another, the rest o' the day, but waited instead, for what, we knew not.

Then just afore dusk, us saw, comin' up to'ards the 'ouse, me mam back. But just 'er. She looks furious as she comes by the 'ouse.

"Where's Granny?" I ask. "Where's Alizon?" And she puts 'er 'and in me face and pushes me out o' the way and back til I bang me 'ead against the wall.

None o' us spoke for some great time within that night. The house seemed bigger and quieter, somehow. I'd never known it without me Gran bein' in it. Me Mam stood, lookin' o'er the cauldron me Gran'd been stirrin', til finally she turns on us. With 'er eyes so askew, it were a frightening thing when she levelled 'er gaze at thee.

"From nah," she said, quakin', "none says a thing about nobody. We mind our own. We don't say nothing that could get each other in trouble to nobody. Nothin'!"

We both nodded. Even James were fearful of 'er when she were in such a mood.

And then there's just the three of us. Wi' both Granny and Alizon gone, no one at 'ome was nice to me. Me mam ranted and raved all day, and she and James would turn on me if I even spoke, so I kept mesen quiet. We waited for word on Alizon and Granny, or for them to just come back one day. I gave over askin' when it might be. I only ever got smacked for that question.

Lancaster Castle. Already back then, they were being borne hence towards this place, along wi' old Chattox, the witch what killed me dad. I wonder sometimes wha' i' were fr 'em, me Gran and Alizon, steppin' through that very door and into this room, me Gran leanin' on Alizon, and lookin' at this terrible place they'd been brought to, thinkin' back on home, wi' us. I wonder if they thought o' me then.

*

Good Friday came. Alizon and Granny gone a week by now, off to wait for their trial at the Lancashire Assizes. We weren't church goers, none o' us, never 'ad been, so Good Friday meant as nothin' to us. I didn't even know it were any special kind o' day at all, not until I woke and smelled the mutton cookin' over the fire in the mornin'. It were that what woke me up, and a want to fill me belly wi' it. We had meat so rare, I were amazed to see it. Me brother James sat by it, tendin' it and lookin' wicked.

"Where's us got this from?" I ask.

"Mind your own," James says. "Anyway, they'll not miss it. Not one sheep, and we've need of it. You've got to feed them what comes in your 'ome if you ask 'em'ere."

"Why?" I asks, "who's comin'?"

But 'e winks at me and taps 'is nose.

By noon, the 'ouse were full of people. Most were women that me Mam seemed to know, but Jane Bulcock had brought her son John. He were a 'andsome lad. Much more 'andsome than me brother James, and he were nice to me, got me to sit reight by him. Whenever 'e'd tear off a piece o' meat off the mutton, 'e'd lean o'er and gi' some to me after.

They all started talking and chattering, all o' 'em, over one another, tearing at the mutton as they went to keep fed. Eventual, me Mam stands to speak above the others.

"You know they've took my girl," says she. "You know they've took my mother wi' 'er. Them what's never done any harm, and Alizon only answerin' a slight of no charity. For this, they've took 'em to Lancaster. To decide whether they've done enough to hang 'em."

"Aye," sayeth one, "they do look for these witches where they may find 'em, and go on lookin' until they do find one. All the time, it's my thinkin', that not a one among them, what they say is a witch, really is. No more a witch than I am this 'ere dead sheep," she says, and she prodded at the mutton.

"Well, they take liberties," another says. She spoke in a funny way, and it were only later that I found that she were from Yorkshire. "You know my time I've 'ad wi' my landlord. Old bugger before 'im wanted me, tried to give me whatever I wanted to lie wi' 'im, but I kept faith. Told 'im, I were a married woman. After 'e died, 'is son tries to run me off me land, worries I'll bring 'is father into disrepute. Said as like I'd gone forth to 'is dad's body and let it bleed afresh from my touch. I've 'alf a mind to find a witch and hex 'im, the son, good and proper. Wouldn't keep me none awake at night to 'ear of 'is passin'!"

"Nay, they say they fear witches, but tis because of Catholics!" yet another'n sayth. "They say that King James is mighty afeared for his life since them what tried to blow him up. Problem is, he wouldn't know a Catholic from a witch, not with his mother bein' both!"

Some tried to comfort my mother, but succeeded only in makin' themselves more angry like she were. They seemed so eager on discussing the cause of Granny's containment, all talking over one another, that they seemed to go on this and none about what they were surely there to discuss. How they might fetch Alizon and my Granny out again. Not til a while later, anyway, when the mutton was nearly gone. One sheep lasts not long between eleven people, I suppose.

"Can we not go to magistrate and plead for 'em?" one suggests.

"No," says John Bulcock sullenly, "we'd need all of Pendle and beyond behind us, as if they do see we're all come home again, them what's us enemies'll see us all be labelled witches."

"Aye," says his mother, also sad. "Then we'll all be at Lancaster Castle, and I've no mind to have me or my son be told by them what don't know us, that we be not Christian folk."

"Aye," me Mam says. "Short of blowin' the place up - and I've nothin' to do so with - and murderin' the gaoler - I've no mind to be hanged - I don't know what to do to fetch em out again."

"What's 'hanged'?" I ask.

Everyone goes quiet and looks at me. "Tha's never seen a hangin', child?"

"She's never 'ad need," me Mam cuts in. "There's no real bad folk round 'ere."

John Bulcock puts 'is arm about me shoulder, and sighs deep. "It's 'ow they punish thee," he says slowly, like he's tryin' to think 'ow best to phrase it as he speaks. "It's 'ow them what's in power, they make sure, if tha's done wrong, that tha'll never be a problem to 'em again."

"Don't go confusin' the child," Jennet Preston, the Yorkshire woman cuts in. "For the sake of goodness - Let's talk o' somethin' else, shall we?"

Eventual, o' course, 'fore it gets too dark, all o' em what's come starts to go again. The same lady what had problems wi' er landlord, this Thomas Lister chap she'd gone on about, she said next time there were a gatherin' among 'em, we should come to 'er house, and she'd feed us all there richly as much as she were able to, and she takes off on this beautiful horse that were little but almost pure white.

I stand wi' me mam, watchin' as she, the last o'em, leaves, and I can feel 'er anger growin' again. Nothing' been decided. No action to be taken. Nothin' to do. Nothin' that can be done. Just wait, like we always do. And she stomps back inside the house.

*

It were dead cold that night. There were a draft comin' from somewhere, curlin' up me back in me little corner, furthest from where the fire normally burnt. And from somewhere above me, a drip-dip started to fall on me, so I woke.

I looked over, in the gloom, to the other side o' the room, where Alizon slept. But o' course, Alizon weren't there, and from hearing everyone earlier, she was unlikely to be home any time soon. So she wouldn't mind, I thought, if, just to get out o' the damp and the cold, I took 'er spot for the night.

I rose and started to creep as quiet as possible o'er to the side, when in the darkness, I hear me mam sit up in bed.

"What's tha doin'?" she demands quietly.

I try and tell 'er, say it were only for the one night, now I know that Alizon won't be back a while. It were drafty and damp in my bit, and just for the night, just Alizon dunt have need -

Somethin' whistles past my ear and crashes into the wall behind me, the clatters to the floor. "Tha'll stay away from where she slept," I heard me mam speak. "She'll come back. She'll come back and take it up again, and if what she's go' is better than thine, then it's because it's for better than thee!"

I make me way back over to my side again, wheepin' as I go. I can 'ear James tryin' not to laugh aloud in the darkness, pretendin' that he'd never woke, but I could 'ear 'im.. And I cried mesen until I slept.

Me mam next day takes some of me Gran's things. An old skull, and some teeth what she'd said were from't local graveyard, and she buries 'em beneath the house. I tried to argue, say they were Granny's things, but she lam'ed me and said we'd all go the way o' Granny and Alizon if we weren't careful.

Days passed again, all rollin' into one another. Granny's seat by the fire cookin' pot were empty, and it felt odd. Alizon never comin' through the door at the end o' the day. None a' 'ome were kind to me now. Mam ranted and raved and James never cared. And then came a knock on the door.
We know by now what happens when there's a knock, and me mam turns to look at James and me in fear and dread: "Both of yer, quickly! Hide!"

She 'ad nowhere to go, and neither of us barely did. James walked into the darkest corner, as if that'd save 'im, and I ducked down behind the only thing that might conceal me, the cauldron.

Then the door bursts opens. Not just the two men this time. More than I could count. They come in and grab me mam by 'er wrists, as she screams in fury at 'em. They spy James almost at once, and grab 'im. He tries to duck away, tries to escape, but it's no good. Each man is big, and broad, and it's nothin' to them to cuff James o'er the head if he tries to evade 'em.

And final, I feel a hand on me shoulder, draggin' me out from behind the cauldron. And I'm so tired. So tired o' all this now. So as me mam shrieks and curses, and James still gets lam'ed o'er the 'ead as 'e tries to get away, I stand with the man what grabbed me, and I walk with him. We've tried the fightin', I reckon. We might as well try somethin' else.

We go on down the road, towards the village a pace, but then us come to a fork, and we go one way, a way I'd never been before. We walk on until we stand outside this grand 'ouse, the like of which I'd never seen. This, the man who walks wi' me says to me, is 'Read Hall', and it's where the Justice Of The Peace, Roger Nowell lives.

It was so large, unlike a house I'd ever seen before! And it seemed to me as nothing that as we went through the front door, me mam went went one way, James another, and then me a third. I were kept in a room with the man what brought me, for what felt like hours. I waited and waited and waited.

Then, at last, the door opens, and I'm ushered through. The room I go through to is larger, wood panellin' on the walls, and facin' me is a table wi' two men behind it. One has a feather in 'is hand, and parchment on the table before him. The other is older, dressed even nicer than the other. he leans across the table to'ards me.

"What is your name, child?" he asks.

"Jennet Device," says I.

"Do you know who I am, Jennet Device?!

"No, sir."

"My name is Roger Nowell. I am the Justice of the Peace in these parts. I am charged with finding if there be witches hereabouts. And this is why I had the brought here today - to help me."

He starts by askin' me questions I can answer fair enough. About mesen, and about me mam, and Alizon, and James, and then me Gran. Then 'e wants to know about Malkin Tower. Wants to know if there were a meeting there on Good Friday. Who were there? Who came? What was said? What was spoken of? Was there much in the way of plans made? Who said what? Was there anythin' strange that happened? Anything I can remember.

I answer as best I might. Then he asks for names of them what were there. He repeats back some names to me. "What about these names, child? Do they mean anythin' to thee?" And he tells me some names. Some are familiar, some not. But he says certain ones again. "How about her, child? You've heard of her, surely?"

"I think so sir."

"And she was there, at Malkin Tower, wasn't she?"

"She might have been, sir."

"Good." And he writes down that name as well. "Alice Nutter," he says at one point. "She would have been there, wouldn't she?"

Now I'd heard of Alice Nutter before, or at least, her family. The Nutters lived down at Roughlee. There were plenty of 'em. They 'ad their own land to live off and everythin'. I didn't reckon I knew Alice Nutter, and I were fairly sure there would 'a' been a To Do 'ad she arrived at Malkin Tower on Good Friday - she were well-thought of. They weren't like noble or nothin', but she wouldn't 'ave 'ad much cause to come and see the likes of us.

"I don't think Alice Nutter was there, sir," I reply.

"Nonsense, child," Mr. Nowell says. "Her family's all Catholics, and she'd be only too eager to go and have conference with witches when all of the King's Faith should have been at church. She was there, wasn't she, Jennet?"

"I don't know, sir," I answer truthfully.

"Well you must know child!" Mr. Nowell, soundin' a bit angry. "And I tell thee, I know Alice Nutter was there. I have it from another that she was, that they saw and spoke to her there. Alice Nutter was there at Malkin Tower at the Good Friday Meeting, wasn't she?"

I thought 'ard. I still weren't sure. "She might 'a' been, sir."

He looks at me level now, and he dunt blink. "She was, child. Wasn't she?"

And even now, I can hear the words tumbling out o' me mouth, unable for me take it back ever after. "Yes, sir. I suppose she must 'a' been."

"Good." And he puts her name down as well. "Is there anything else to tell me? Anything that you know of your family to tell? Anything that might help me in my discovery of witches. Think hard, child. What can thou say?"

Nobody'd ever asked me such a question afore. So I tell 'im. I tell 'im what I know. I tell 'im about Granny, and Old Chattox, and she'd made me dad die, and Alizon's curse was not meant, though she should've minded 'er words, and about me mam and odd things me brother's said that might make 'im a witch for all I know, and I start to say some o' it, like reciting things I'd 'eard the rest o' em say.

And Mr. Roger Nowell never interrupts me once. He sits amazed, and a smile starts to creep up 'is face the more I talk. And when I don't know what else to say, I'm silent.

"Well, Jennet. I've enough here to be able to do my work for now, thou's been very been kind in helping me. Art thou hungry? Come through and we'll have us something to eat, so if we need work any further, we can do so on full stomachs."

He took me through into another room, where there were plates of food waitin' for us. It were the biggest lot of food I'd ever seen in all me life. It was piping hot, and made my stomach rumble to look on it. When my plate was loaded up, I asked:

"Is all this for me?" and Mr. Nowell laughed at me. I didn't even know what some of it were, but I ate it. It tasted so delicious, better'n anythin' I'd 'ad before in all me life. I could barely move afterward, I ate so much. And all the while, Mr. Nowell grins to see me eat so heartily.

When we're done eatin', I were half asleep for satisfaction, and Mr. Nowell says:

"Does thou like it here, Jennet? This food and this warmth?"

I answer that I do, very much. It's been a cold enough winter past, and I reckon aloud that I've not seen so much food as this inside a month past.

"Well," he says, "I'd like to see thy life better than it has been. You're a good, clever girl, aren't you, Jennet? I reckon as your family's not so good to thee as I am now. Thee up in Malkin Tower, youngest. Do they treat thee well, Jennet?"

I do not answer. I remember what it is to go to bed with my brother thumpin' me for no reason. Me mam's fury. The cuts and the bruises and the empty belly. How my not bringing back enough as the others is a frightful thing to me, but I had nowhere else to go but 'ome...

"If thou wants a better life, Jennet, you'll not get one up in Malkin Tower with witches about thee. None'll touch thee. Jesus Himself won't touch thee, child, and I hate to think of a child like thee in Damnation."

And he tells me more of Jesus, and Paradise, and Perdition, that which I've only half-heard before, and I grow afeared from what 'e says, for knowin' my family, be they witches, I'm not like to come near the Gates of Paradise.

"But there is hope for thee yet, Jennet, and I mean to save thee, be it the last thing I may do..."

*

Four months, I stayed with Mr. Nowell. Even now when I look back on it, knowing what I know and what I didn't know then, them days, they were easily the happiest days of my life.

I loved Read Hall. I never knew such favour. Mr. Nowell didn't make me go out and beg, and he said that I could make use of whatever I liked in the house, and it would not be stealin', because I was 'is guest. I slept in a bed each night, my own bed, not in a damp and drafty corner, and nobody told me to move, or bothered me.

The only thing Mr. Nowell wanted was for me to talk. Again, and again, every evenin', telling 'im the answers to the questions he put to me, or speakin' on my own. Sometimes, I was given rest, and he would read to me from his book on Deamonologie, which 'e said was written by the king himself, and it helped him better identify witches. Told you the kind of thing to look for, and 'ow to trick 'em, and be wise to their ploys.
People came and went from the house a lot, givin' 'im news and talkin', and sometimes they stopped to speak to me. One gave Mr. Nowell a paper one time, then before passin' me, he smiled at me, or tried to smile. Mr. Nowell pushed the paper away, like he didn't want me to read it, even though I can't read.

Do you know, if it meant me staying with Mr. Nowell in his lovely house for as long as I could, then I'd 'a' done anything. Food like that every night, a nurse to bathe me and sleeping in comfort?. I'd 'a' done anything.

One night, as I sat before the fire warmin' mesen, I looked up at Mr. Nowell and said:

"Mr. Nowell. Wha' about me Granny? Me Granny did nothin' wrong, sir. She's not bad, even if she's a witch. Can she come here sometime? I'd like that. I could look after 'er! Better than me mam ever did."

Mr. Nowell was smokin' of 'is pipe and 'e said to me: "After the trial, maybe."

"I don't want to get 'er in trouble. She won't be in trouble, will she? Not me Gran. She's not bad."

He smiled awkwardly, and there were a knock at the door. We went to answer it, and a man were standin' in the rain, with words written on a page. Mr. Nowell read it over and grinned, then came inside again.

"Jennet Preston's been hanged in Yorkshire," he said to me. "Well done, child."

I recognised the name. She, I realised, 'ad been there on the Good Friday Meeting. She'd had the white foal-horse. She'd been the lady from Yorkshire, what had spoken of 'er landlord. "She's been punished then, sir?" I asked.

"Aye. It's done," he said, and he went to bed, rubbin' 'is hands together.

It felt like a long time at the time, but four month went by quick. Then Mr. Nowell says the time 'as come, and we're off to Lancaster to tell others about Good Friday. We went in this carriage, the only one I'd ever been in before.

I never knew how big the world might be, and Mr. Nowell laughed at me, gazin' from the window at everythin' I saw, and askin' where we were from time to time, and could we come again and look better later? We stayed overnight in an inn, and then, in the mornin', I finally caught me first glimpse of Lancaster Castle.

It were the largest place ever I'd seen before. I were nervous as we went in. You see, Mr. Nowell 'ad warned me that the rest of 'em would be there - they had to be, so 'e said. I 'adn't seen me mam, me Granny, or any of 'em in months, but I was still so young it might as well 'ave been forever, and me life were so different now. But Mr. Nowell walked so confident with me, I tried to put it aside. He left and said he'd come fetch me when I was needed.

I waited a while. I 'eard snatches of voices on the other side of the door where I were waitin'. Sounded like me sister, Alizon. Sounded like 'er cryin', like she'd break 'er 'eart wi' weepin'. Then another voice. Not contrite, this. Not cryin' or sorry-like. This voice was angry, and shoutin', and I knew it, and I feared it. It were me mam. Callin' that she'd done nothin', they were lyin', she were an innocent woman. Made me shake. And then the door opened and Mr. Nowell called me to come in.

The room I went into were large, ceilin' high above me head. All these people were in there, dead quiet. I'd 'a' never known there were so many people for 'ow quiet it was on the outside. Then, when they see me, they set to chatterin' with one another, like I were a strange thing. There's these two men with funny lookin' hair, then there's people in normal or nice dress in the room, and then there's another bit, separate. And there at the front is me mam.

As me mam looks on me, her face goes white, and I wished at once that I'd not come forth. She screams at me, with a sound that makes the room cave in about me. "Jennet!" she screams, top of 'er voice. And she shouts, cries, curses, and I've never seen 'er so angry. "Damn thee, bastard!" she screams at Mr. Nowell. "I'll see thee in thy grave for this!" Then she screams at everyone: "How dare you bring my daughter to speak against me!" She goes on and on, gettin' louder, and I start to cry - I can't 'elp it, I've always been afraid of 'er.

I know I cannot speak with 'er there to listen to me, and I'll never be 'eard above her. So with my tears, I speak to them two what sits in front of all, and point at mam, askin' that she be taken away, for then I can speak. "Let 'er be taken," I cry, "and then I can speak! But please, take her forth, I can't speak with 'er 'ere!"

Me mam taken, the judges nod towards this table set up, and because I'm still small, I climb upon it so all might see me. So strange it was, to be looked on by so many. I looked for me Gran in their number, for I could see Alizon, and James, 'im lookin' like 'e'd been taken ill, but me Gran weren't there.

I stood on the table, tall as I could get, and I began to speak:

"My mother is a witch, and that I know to be true…"

*

"Guilty of causing death or harm by witchcraft.

"Elizabeth Device. Alizon Device. James Device. Anne Whittle, Anne Redfern. Isabel Robey. Alice Nutter. Jane Bulcock. John Bulcock. Katherine Hewitt."

Two days I'd spoken and answered questions put to me. I'd spoken of my mother, and the spirit sent forth. Told of my brother James, and how he had been a witch for three years, and how each of 'em had been sent out to kill others. Went alongside those who were there on Good Friday, and those who were not, and had to pick out the guests from the absent, from prisoners of the castle, but to be sure that I was right in my accusation. I just picked 'em out from who'd been there in the dock before. Weren't 'ard a' all. Twice the judges fed me names I did not know to trip me up, but I stayed true, and Mr. Nowell looked pleased every time. They let several witches go, from Salmesbury, what 'ad been accused and abused, it would seem, but my lot...

The judge puts this black thing, like a flat kind o' cap on his wig and then speaks: "Hence to the castle from whence you came...to the place of execution..." And I heard no more, for Mr. Nowell was takin' me out the room again.

"Well done, child," says he with a grin. I've never seen 'im look so pleased.

"Am I done now?" I ask, pleasantly surprised. "Can I go see me Granny now?"

He falters, but keeps grinnin'. "After tomorrow, Jennet," he says. "After tomorrow.."

*

I remember that day at Gallows Hill like I'll never remember any other day like it. There were so many there that day, on the outskirts o' town, pushing and shovin', and I were only little. Mr. Nowell had a hold of my hand as we first climbed, but I couldn't keep up, and then my wrist slipped from 'is grip. I tried to catch up, but 'e were too quick for me. I struggle and try to make my way, until a man spies me.

"Does tha want to see the hangin', child?" he asks me.

I nod, and he puts me on his shoulders so I can see.

I see the gallows some little way off. There's a strong beam, and ropes 'angin' from 'em. Then beneath, there they all are, standin' in a cart with their 'ands tied, behind those circles of rope. A man in a black mask which does cover his face is putting the hoops about their necks, one b' one.. How strange their faces look. Some are sad or angry and some just look tired, or as if they're still asleep but with their eyes open. Some o' 'em dunt even look like they're awake a' all, which I think in that moment is a shame, cuz it's such a nice day. Alizon is cryin', showin' her teeth in a smile through it, which makes no sense. James is still ill. He looks so white in the face, and he can barely stand. The man whose shoulders I sit on turns to her what's with 'im and says: "There's must be that James Device. Word was 'e tried to do himself away while he were in the prison, but they weren't 'avin' it. I'm glad 'e's 'ere today instead."

Then there's me Mam. She looks out o'er people, but I've never seen 'er look like that before. Like, she's not thinkin' or feelin' anythin'. Just starin'.

Then there's a man in a long dress, what is white, and 'e 'olds a book wi' 'im. He goes from person to person in the cart just by it, talkin' to 'em. Some pay 'im mind, some don't. But when e' gets to me man, she won't even look at 'im. He gives a nod towards the man at the front of the cart with the horse and slowly, ever so slowly, the cart begins to move beneath them.

Isabel Robey is the first to fall. She falls suddenly, tryin' to keep her balance on the cart and resistin' it, she falls further. There's this great snap, and she bounces on the end of the rope, and her 'ead falls to one side, in a way I've never seen a head do. Then another falls, must be John Bulcock. He shouts somethin' just before he falls, but the word 'alf comes out before his eyes bulge and his tied, useless hands are grabbin' at his neck, as if he might free himsen. His mother, Jane, were standin' right by, and as her son falls, she screams. She screams this horrible, shriekin' scream, like for a moment she weren't even human at all, and it comes up from right inside her, this scream, and everyone in the crowd is silent now, just listening to her call out.

And that were the first moment. I suddenly knew somethin' were wrong. This was punishment? But this was… This was… What was this? What were I seein'?

Jane Bulcock reaches out, like to grab her son John, and falls hersen off the end of the cart, and starts swingin' next to him, her mouth opening and shutting. 'Er son tries to reach out to 'er, his tied, useless hands goin' to 'er - 'is neck - to 'er - 'is neck… Alice Nutter, she grabs onto the side of the cart and starts crying out to all gathered that they're innocent, they've done nothing wrong, they're murdering innocent people. Katherine Hewitt goes to follow Alice's lead, but then she falls. There's a horrible splatterin' as she does, and something falls out from under her dress, like bits from inside her.

What is this? is all I can think. I can't understand it. These people are fallin', and then not movin', and somethin's changed. What is this? This is punishment, this is…

Old Chattox is muttering, huddlin' in wi' 'er daughter Anne, right beside her, just as Alice Nutter, still trying to free hersen falls off, bumping into Katherine Hewitt as she goes, Alice Nutter's mouth growing wide and ridiculous, trying to take in big gulps of air. Anne Redfearne and Old Chattox, they fall together, mother and daughter, and Anne's still lookin' at her mam, and there's tears all over her face.

Then James collapses at the bottom of the cart, can't stand up none no more, for the rope int that long. And Alizon's screaming, almost as bad as Jane Bulcock for her son, and tryin' to get close to me mam for protection.

And last is me mam. And I realise suddenly, like I hadn't known before, that she's lookin' at me. Looking reight at me, with that look of nothin' on her face. I don't know how long she'd been starin', but her face barely changes as she falls along wi' Alizon, and they're the last of 'em.

This great cry, like a cheer, goes up from all them what's around, then the big man takes me off his shoulders and puts me on the ground and he, along with everyone else, starts to leave. Like nothin' 'ad ever 'appened. They just go, and leave us all there, until I can see plain mesen, all the way to them gallows, and all of them, hangin' from it.

Some of Alice Nutter's folk have come. I 'eard them when she fell, but now, they rush forward and they're shrieking and crying and pullin' on her legs, gettin' 'old of 'er skirts, pullin' on 'er hard. She's not even gone yet.

I just stood there, lookin'. Hanged. So this is what it was. Alice Nutter bein' dead now, them as what pulled her move across and see me mam's still alive, still twitchin' and they move to'ards her… They start on her. And I wanted to tell 'em to stop it, to leave 'er alone, or run and fetch someone to, cut 'er down before she went white like James, before stuff fell out of her, before she went blue like the rest of 'em. And I started to shout a little, can't remember what I said. But they didn't listen. They just pulled… And even afterwards, when I knew, somehow, that her eyes were just starin' now, and she couldn't see anything, she still seemed to be lookin' at me.

I wandered about the field a bit. Still couldn't find Mr. Nowell, and I was fearful because I did not know the way back to 'is house, but I saw a man dressed like they seemed to be at the Castle, so I ran to 'im and said the first thing that were in m' 'ead.

"Can I see my Granny now?"

He looked down at me as if confused. "Granny?" he repeats. "How's tha mean?"

"Me Granny," I said again. "I've done now, so Mr. Nowell said I had to wait til after it were over for me to see her."

"Who's Granny supposed to be?"

"Demdike," I inform him. "Granny Demdike, please let me see her. She's old, really old, and she can't see reight well. I want to take her home and visit her at Malkin Towers."

He shakes his head. "You mean the eldest o' them witches? Elizabeth Southerns, that's who you mean, in't it?"

"Yes, that's 'er," I said hopefully.

"Has no one told thee? She's dead, girl. She were dead weeks ago. Died in that same cell what they pu' 'er in."

Everyone was nearly gone. I waited a bit to see what 'appened to all them what'd been hanged. They were slung back in the cart, and I ran after it. It smelled funny. My sister's arms were hanging down at the back and I ran to grab her 'and. She were cold, and really white. The cart rattled some little way, to where men with spades stood, and they start to all chuck them in the ground. And not one of 'em moved. They couldn't. They'd been - hanged.

I ran back down the hill, calling for Mr. Nowell, who would not leave without me. And I ran, and I knew nobody. I came to a cart what had some people I thought I knew from the village nearby, and I asked the driver if he were goin' near Pendle. He looked at me funny, then brought me up front with him. Some people saw me and hushed. We were in silence the entire way back, and it took all day.

I were the last get off. It were nearly completely dark when I got back to Read Hall. I jumped down, and the cartman told me he could take me back to Malkin Tower if I wanted, it were only a little further, but I told him, no, here was fine. And I knocked on the door. Nothin'. Not for ages, but the chimney were goin' and there were light from within, so he must have got back already. I shivered in the growin' cold, and still the door was not opened.

But I hammered on the door til I thought my fists would bleed, and finally, Mr. Roger Nowell stands in the doorway. His look to me is changed, though.

"What's amiss, child?" 'e says with a laugh begging to creep between his lips. "More witches, is it?"

I dunt know what to make of what he says. "No... I did what I was asked. I said all the things tha said I should say - I said 'em perfect, I never made a mistake, and now it's done."

"Aye, it's done," he says. "And what do you want wi' me?"

I didn't answer him at first. He'd asked me how I liked his house, and I'd liked it well, but now, he barred my way in. "You said I should have a better life." I don't like the way he looks at me now. "If I did as tha said, it would be much better for me."

"And do you not think it is, child?" he speaks. "All the witches that plagued thy life are gone now. Thou hast Malkin Tower all thy own. And I do reckon upon none in Pendle or beyond shall try and take from thee what's thine, not now they know thou's had people hanged for as much."

I stood blinkin' at 'im.

"Jennet," he says. "Think clearly, child. I am a respectable man. I cannot be seen to be take in bastard children of witches." And the door shuts in my face.

A hand upon my shoulder startles me, but it's just the driver. Without a word, 'e takes me back to the cart and drives me home. Malkin Tower.

Strange to be back again. Everythin' was just as we'd left it, that day when the men burst through the door, all those months ago. Everythin' the same. Even the food in cauldron, what had long gone off and smelled so bad. But it were gettin' cold outside, so I settled down in me little corner, leavin' the space for everyone else, as if they'd have need of it again. Even though... I were all that were left now.

*

Next morn, I were sick. Not eaten since day before, I realise. So I go towards the village, lookin' for someone to ask food from. But none was willin' to give like they 'ad before. They'd look at me odd, then move along, quicker. Like I weren't even there at all.

I tried all day to get somethin', even runnin' after people I knew, but they acted like they couldn't see me. And I stood with nothin' in my hands, and my stomach groanin' wi' hunger, willin' to do anythin' to get a little somethin'. I missed those big meals I'd have at Mr. Nowell's house, but I didn't need that much. A cut of bread or an apple. But I didn't reight have the strength to go to the orchard. I felt as I'd fall before I got there, then -

"Jennet?" says a voice, a man's voice, what's stopped nearby. I turn to 'im.

He stands afore me, lookin' strange familiar, in a way. An elder man - elder than me mam, not as old as me Granny.

"It's Jennet Device, int it?" And now I remember his face. He were one o' them what truly were at Malkin Tower on that Good Friday, his name bein' Christopher, and me mam sayin' that he were uncle to me. He looks at me in amazement as I stand with nothin' in me 'ands to show for all me day.

He takes me by the shoulders wi' sayin' nothin', and off we go through a little part of the village til he comes to a little house, pushes open the door and in we go. The lady sat there I recognise also. Also were she one at Malkin Tower that day, and she sits up in 'er chair, terrified at the site of me.

"By the Almighty," she says, and crosses herself. "This cannot be…"

"It is," he replies over my 'ead. "It's Jennet, our Elizabeth's girl. She were out beggin' as were they wont out near the market. They've put her like this, made no provision for 'er."

She smiles as if she's tryin' to mean it. "The poor little child," says she, and gives me a cut of bread, which I finish quick enough. I hear 'er talkin' to Uncle Christopher as I do.

"She can't stay 'ere, Christopher, love, tha knows she can't. She what's been bought easy enough before, or is so easy swayed, can be so again, and the likes of the law are not them what'll take pity on us if she speaks against us."

"Don't talk so soft," says he to her as I finish me bread. "She's a babe. She were used worst of all. Let's at least feed 'er today and see what us can do tomorrow."

They let me stay that night before the little fire that they have there. After Elizabeth, me aunt of sorts, 'as gone to bed, me uncle sits wi' me and says nary a thing for a lang time, then at last he speaks:

"Tweren't thee, Jennet Device. Tweren't thee. Tha weren't to know. That all them what came for'ard and said as like me mam, and your mam, and the Chattoxes might have done some 'arm, that all o' 'em 'ad some gripe. Them's wanted their land. Them's wanted her off their land. Truth is, they all spoke against each other as well. Our lot spoke against the Chattoxes for thieving from us some years back, and for your dad's death, just like the Chattoxes had out for us because she reckoned me old mam had been where she shouldn't a been, had wronged her. Was tha there, when they all were 'anged?"

I answered I 'ad been.

"I'm reight glad I did not see that. Reight glad. To 'ang babes alongside old women as can't defend 'emselves before the law. It's not reight. I tell thee, it's not reight…" And 'e goes off to bed cryin'.

In truth, I weren't there a night. I were there several. Me aunt Elizabeth said I'd got plump off livin' at Mr. Nowell's 'ouse and gettin' used to 'is good food, and I suppose I had, but I couldn't stay. A few days later, me uncle Christopher takes me back up to Malkin Tower. He says I may as well sleep in the nice part o' the house now, where me mam and Granny's sleep, as there's none'll stop me. He sures up the door so that when I'm out or within, none can get in without me lettin' em. Shows me how best to make fire and put it out again. Says he'll bring some food when he's able, but I've gotta look after mesen now. He tells me places wha' occasionally 'ave more and if I'm sneaky, I can get mesen some.

Just afore 'e goes, he stands in't field beyond the door, showin' me where'd be good spots for me to plant seeds for the like of food 'e'll bring me, and he'll tell me how and when, and a woman appears. She's marchin' o'er wi' a face like thunder, and she levels 'er gaze on me, and looks fit to murder me. She's older, but not like Granny, and she's filthy, bu' 'er face is red. Me uncle 'as to stop 'er from gettin' at me.

"Let me 'ave at 'er, let me at the little child of the devil!" she screams. "Let me tear 'er, wring 'er neck! Let 'er suffer, same as my ald mother 'ad to, same as my sister wi' er." From this I know now, not knowin' before, this is a daughter of Old Chattox.

"Calm thesen, Elizabeth Whittle!" me uncle says, for though they're of an age, 'e's still a strong man and 'olds 'er back. From 'is callin' 'er Whittle, I realise that this is Old Chattox's real name, so this must be 'er other daughter. "Not do thee any good, nor good for thy mother nor sister neither, not to 'arm a little child what's been used like the rest 'o 'em."

"Not do good!" she shrieks. "I'm no' 'ere to do good! My neice wi'out her mam nar, 'er dad wi'out his wife. It were 'er brother and sister what spoke against my mother, what never did either o' them any 'arm, and she said no words about 'em! Let me at the little child, one less Device is all I need to 'ave peace o' mind."

"Then thy arguments wi' the siblin's, not wi' er! And what, tha wants to 'ave at her for them already bein' dead? Go on then! 'Ave at her, then, and see if it stops there. You see if from there, she be the last of us to die!"

At this, this lady, Elizabeth Whittle, she falls to the ground, crying and weepin' aloud to sound around the valley. "My mother's dead," she weeps, her mouth barely lettin' her lips meet. "My mother and sister's dead! Not warm and comfortable in their bed, with us to bring them peace about 'em. Mocked! Made to suffer, suffer so bad…"

"And tha'll have it on 'er, will tha?" says Christopher. "'Er, wi' grandmother to 'er and mother to me, dead first? Then 'er mother and my sister, my niece and nephew, 'er brother and sister, all o' them gone, but it's this child tha wants murder against?"

She cries a little more, then Uncle Christopher picks 'er up and takes 'er back the way she came, shoutin' at me that 'e'll be back to see me soon.

I watched 'em go. It frightened me almost as much as That Day had. I wondered how many thought as she did, Old Chattox's daughter. That they blamed me for them what 'ad not come 'ome, what 'ad 'appened to 'em. Me for sayin' names and speakin' all I knew, not bein' nothin' but sayin' what I were told. I wondered how many people, though they mayn't say, wanted to murder me, just like that man with the cart 'ad murdered all them what 'ad been in it.

*

Me uncle Christopher were as good as 'is word, and he came by wi' food a bit, tellin' me not to eat it all at once, not while he comes again, but I usually do. Eat mesen silly, then have nothing for days at a time. I miss warm food and comfy beds, but I slowly to live past 'avin' 'ad 'em, and knowin' I'll never get 'em again.

Sometimes, me uncle couldn't make it out so well, but he feared for me, so 'e sent a boy from the village. William Nutter. Little older than me. I never knew 'ow 'e was cousin to Alice, but they all 'ave kinship with one another somehow.

When 'e first came, I only saw 'is back. There were a knock at the door and by the time I'd gone to answer it, he were halfway down the 'ill, this pile of vegetables in the doorway. Then me uncle must 'a' asked how I were, for William stopped in a bit, to ask me how I were, did I need anythin' doin'. I didn't, and William took off again, like a lightening flash. Little by little, he got bolder. Stopped and talked to me longer. One day, I said I were makin' broth, and would 'e like some 'ere 'e go. 'E said 'e would, and in 'e comes for the first time.

'E looks about the place as 'e sits down, says it's a queer thing, to see a little girl in among the place by hersen. We make snatches of the bread he's brought me warm and crisp before the fire I've made. He grows bold at last, and asks:

"Were it a fright?" he asks me. "Livin' wi' witches?"

I stir of the cauldron. "No," I say. "Not a fright. It were like...livin' wi' family."

"Your Uncle says they were no witches. That it were all a lie. That 'is mother were just an old woman what were used. Is it true?"

And I don't answer 'im. I keep my peace.

"They say, int village, that it were thy words what took 'em to the gallows. Is that right too?"

Again, I say nothin'. I feel like somethin's caught in me throat.

"He told me... That it weren't your fault though. That you were tricked as much as any of 'em. That they made thee say it. Is that what 'appened, Jennet? They made thee say it, din't they?"

And I started crying. Since that day, I'd not cried. But I cried then, so hard I couldn't stand up. And William put his arm about me. It was the closest I've felt to anyone in all my life.

But they'd died. All o' 'em. They'd died. Some of 'em for comin' to see me mam on Good Friday, some for merely knowin' 'er, some for me and James knowin' their names better than others, and so at so little in age, it were in my mind like me and the man in the mask, or 'im what guided the cart, like them and I had traded places, and it'd been me what said they were ready for 'anging, me wha' took the support aat from under the' feet until all o' 'em were swingin'...

*

I only went out to beg if it were really bad for me. Thanks to me uncle, and William, it weren't. I soon 'ad my own little crop goin', but in the colder times, when there was no crop, I 'ad to beg. This one time, I were in the village and this carriage starts to go by. I try to hop on, and I thrust me 'and inside.

The man inside looks at me quick, then sighs and takes his purse, droppin' some coin into me 'and. And we stop. And we look. And we recognise each other.

I drop down from the carriage as it trundles along. And I wanted to shout after Mr. Roger Nowell. Wanted to ask 'im 'Why?' But instead, I dropped the coins in the dirt for someone else to find 'em.

At least 'is fortune 'ad improved no more than mine. They'd forgotten about 'im, same as he had me, once all were dead, and I were a little pleased to see a man who thought himself so fine had not found his betterment.

*

My Uncle came less and less as 'e grew. Gettin' old, he were. Barely saw 'im, but William in 'is place. 'E'd set to puttin' things reight if anythin' were off for me. 'E didn't complain neither. As 'e found I never hexed 'im, 'e trusted me more, and 'e'd stay longer, sometimes most o' the day, at Malkin Tower. On one of 'is visits, William says to me: "There's a bloke int' village what's askin' for thee. Asked me if tha looked like tha sister, Alizon."

"Do I, then?"

"No, not really," William says. "I told 'im so. He says 'e don't mind, and 'e wants to come see thee anyway."

"Wants to come see me, what for?" I asks.

"Don't know. Reckon 'e wants to sleep wi' thee. Asked if I 'ad and if it were any good. I said I didn't know anythin'. So he tells me to ask thee if he can come."

"No, 'e can't," says I. "I've got best spot in the 'ouse now, I'm not givin' it to someone else what wants to sleep 'ere."

William tuts and rolls 'is eyes at me. "No," he says. "It's not like that. It's like, yer layin' down next to each other, and yer start 'avin' a fight. But it's a nice fight, so yer keep 'avin' it."

"'Ow can you 'ave a nice fight?"

"'e says 'e'll give thee money for it, or give thee a chicken or summat."

"I'm not 'avin' a figh' wi' nobody!" says I, and thanks be, we don't talk about i' again.

Me uncle took me to church a couple o' times, on the important days, like All Saints Day, and Yuletide. Good Friday. 'E were like a dad to me, and I never known me own. 'E always looked out for me, though. 'E'd turn up if 'e were worried, or William'd come to my door. Reckon I'd not be alive if it weren't for me Uncle Christopher, really.

A few years 'ad passed, and I were growin' even more, when I realised I 'adn't seen me uncle in awhile, so I took mesen down to 'is 'ouse in the village. But when I knocked on the door, it were just me aunt Elizabeth inside, and she wouldn't let me in, and she were cryin'. I takes mesen into the village lookin' for 'im still, and I see William there, whose face goes pale to look on me. He turned me about and takes me 'ome. He's older now, like me. As we get just outside the 'ouse, I look on him, and think 'ow handsome he looks these days. Then 'e tells me:

"Tha'll not see Mr. 'Olgate no more. He died in 'is bed, reight peaceful I reckon, 'bout a fortnight ago. There were a funeral. I were gonna come and fetch thee, but Mrs. 'Olgate said I were not to. I'm sorry, Jennet." He puts 'is arms around me,, like 'e did that time before, and then he's gone. And everyone's dead all over again.

*

Years passed, as they always do. Few bothered me, save for William. Bought all his vegetables from me, else I'd have prob'ly starved. I 'ad little to do with anyone else. I heard most of what was goin' on in the village, the older I grew, through William when 'e'd come see me now and again.

"'E's dead," says William one day.

"Who's dead?"

"Roger Nowell. That magistrate man. I 'eard it the other day. Died last week. Though tha'd want to know."

"Right," says I. "Good of thee to tell me."

"I'm gettin' married, Jennet."

"Oh. Who to?"

"Her name's Isabel."

"I see. Is she pretty, this Isabel?"

"Pretty enough, I suppose. She's not reight strong. Not like thee… Jennet, I can't come as much as I'd like no more. Things'll be thought what aren't true. Tha knows what they call this place. Tha knows what they say of thee in the village and even beyond. They talk about this place as if there still be witches here e'en now. We neither of us can get in trouble. Do you see what I mean?"

He wouldn't 'a' ever married me, anyway. Who wants to marry the bastard child of a witch?

William came to see me less, but he still came when 'e could get away. Reckon 'e feared me uncle's ghost if 'e did not. Time just goes on. Years maybe. Then William's at my house one night. He sits before the fire, thinkin' really deep and quiet for ages. Then finally:

"No children. Years gone by, and still no children for Isabel and me… Jennet. Does tha remember some things that Granny Demdike did?"

"Like what?"

"You know. Things she'd give people, to make 'em better."

I know already what he'll ask me. "I remember bits of it, I suppose. Long time ago, mind."

"Aye," he says, "but… if there were anything I could get thee, so tha could make something for her. Tha could do it, couldn't tha? Tha could 'elp us have a child."

And it 'appened just as I knew it would. I didn't just 'elp William's wife. I 'elped William when 'e were sick. I 'elped the girl on my doorstep some weeks after. Some of 'em I just didn't know, and they went away empty-handed, but for what I could remember, I weren't livin' so worried for starvin'. Isabel got better, stronger, but every time they thought a child would come, it would not. 'E'd turn up in my door, in the middle o' the night sometimes, lookin' tired. Sometimes I wanted to just grab 'im and say: 'Let me have it for thee', but 'e'd never 'a' done it.

*

More time passes. People come and go now, leave me things when I 'elp 'em, just like Gran. I get by easier. Then one day I'm hoeing in my garden, and I can 'ear someone coming. This man, and wi' 'im, is a little boy, round-eyed and thin. Seen neither of 'em before.

"I wanted to show my son where witches live," the man calls over to me.

"That's bold of thee," I shout back. "Most stay away for that reason! Besides, there's no witches 'ere now. Not for more'n twenty year, by my reckonin'."

"Aye, aye," he says, then: "It's Jennet Device, int it? They said it might be thee what lives 'ere now."

"I do," says I, puttin' down my hoe. "What does tha really want?"

"Nowt," he says. "Nothin'. As I say, for my son to see. Sad though, int it, that people reckon there might still be witches 'ere now. Rumours is that tha's more like tha family than anyone knows, because they see so little o' thee. T'would be such a shame if tha were accused, like tha mother."

I grip the hoe in my hand. "Tha's usin' me," I realised. "Take theesen away, and take tha son wi' thee."

"Or what?" he asks with a grin. "Tha'll hex me?"

"Oh no," says I. "Running thee off with this hoe will be so much faster. Now take theesen away."

He turned at that, but only to move a little away.

"Friends with William Nutter, aren't tha? Word is tha love him."

I felt like knocking his teeth from his head.

"Sad about his wife though, int it?" he called.

"How's that? What's sad, she lost another child?"

"Oh no," he said. "She's dead," and he took the child's hand and off they walked, wi' never a look back at me. What was he accusing me of?

Everyone I ever took any o' dislikin' to is dead, I thought. Maybe even Isabel Nutter. Poor William.

The man's words stuck with me though. Worryin' about what they say around Pendle and beyond. So I did the only thing I knew to do for't' best. Next Sabbath, I made sure I went to church.

I didn't know hardly any of the songs all the others seemed to know, but I hummed bits when I knew the tune, and people seemed to smile at me, like they could see that I were tryin'. Tryin' my best. It didn't feel like it 'ad though. Maybe they'd forgotten by now. It were so many years ago, after all. It didn't feel like they feared me. And for just a moment, I reckoned, maybe I could come back. Start to come more into the village, 'ave friends and maybe even work for someone.

Then everything stops a minute. The same little boy what that man'd had with him outside my house stood up on a table at the front o' the congregation. Really unnervingly, 'is round eyes peered out towards everyone. His father comes to 'is side and whispers in his ear. The little boy nods. He looks here, and there. Then his finger comes out. He points at one, a woman in the front row. Then another, along the aisle. And finally, his eyes fall upon me, and slowly, deliberately, he points towards me.

Me mouth goes dry, me throat like ash. What does 'e mean? His father takes him down again and we, all in confusion, look one to the other, as if to ask what any of it might mean.

I took mesen home without speakin' to anyone else. Not goin' back, I thought. No goin' back now. But what did it mean? They 'ad nothin' against me, surely. Most o' it would just be gossip, nothin' sure. But what did 'e want? Why point at me?

And who'd really believe the words of a little child?

And in the middle o'f the night, the knock, like a dream from long ago, came on the door at Malkin Tower.

"I'm ready," says I.

*

They put questions to me, like they'd done before, but now I saw a different side to it all. I'm asked about mesen. I'm asked about others. I'm asked about what I've given, what I've made, and for whom. Then they try to make me talk. Keep me up at night. Don't let me be fed, do all things the way they must have tortured my family into sayin' what they said, only to make the pain stop, and I thought of it so many times! They tried their best to break me. They even told me Isabel Nutter 'ad spoke on 'er deathbed that I must've cursed 'er, for want o' William. And that William believed her. But this time, I were wise. I knew the wiliness of the courts now. Like a game for them, and I knew the minute I gave them an inch, told them that maybe I'd done something, my eyes'd stare out from my head the same way my mother's did that day, and I'd see nothing. So his time, I held my tongue, said nothin', rememberin' me mother's words what I should 'a' listened to all them years before. 'We don't say nothin'. We mind our own.' And I took the pain, and the not-sleepin', and the starvin' and them takin' me apart to look at me secrets and prod me, and I trusted no one. And I said nothin'.

One night, the door opens and William comes in. He looks reight well, but a bit sad. And 'e sits wi me. "Did you do it, Jennet?" he asks.

"William Nutter," I answer with what voice I have. "Even if I knew how, for what reason would I cause you such needless pain, of all people?"

He tried to smile, then he got up and he left. I never saw 'im again.

It were only a matter o' time before they brought me 'ere. There were about twenty of us to begin, I were just one of a number. And they bring out this boy again, and others to accuse each other. And I wanted to shout 'Stop it, the lot of yer! Does none of yer realise it's all 'appened before?.' But of course, I'd be condemning misen, so I continue to keep me peace. They'll not make me say nothin' no more. Even when I spoke now, me voice just sounded like me mam's.

But this judge was different. Not like for my lot. He looked on as the stories were told as if he had no more taste for what was said, than he had for eatin' muck for dinner. "I cannot find, in good prudence, this evidence to my liking. I hear call for the matters to be heard by one higher than myself, and let their decision be made."

The boy, Edmund Robinson, were taken down to London to be spake at by others to know 'is story better. Stranger still, they took some o' us wi' em. Not me, I were left behind, but I heard what happened when they'd returned. They'd been shown off. People paid a penny to see the great witches of Lancashire, and then they'd go see one o' them pretendings that apparently they do at a place called playhouse, what reckons they know all about us story. I'm glad I weren't among their number. Not to be looked and wondered at, not again.

Some o' em came back in more fear than when they went, for people had spoke in front o'em like they couldn't be heard.

"There's a place called Bohemia," said one girl wi' the shakes. "The Quen there, she dunt have the witches hanged… She 'as them burnt. But they say they do the same up in Scotland as well!" And I were reight pleased then to be an Englishwoman. I would get enough flame in Perdition. I did not need it as me dyin' method. Best wi' the life choked out of thee either quick or to have them what takes pity on thee yankin' to bring thee to thy death happily, not to be burnt, not like some piece o' meat.

One night, one o' them guards what still comes regular along this corridor is makin' a noise to raise 'dead. "Hush up, can't thee?" I shout at 'im. "Let us get some peace for all that we don't otherwise get!"

He continues, singin' and runnin' 'is tankard along the bars, 'til I come to the door. "Hush!" I shout out. "Hush or I'll curse thee, tha drunken base-born!"

"I know tha'll not 'urt me," he says. "Tha's not a witch."

"What? What does tha mean? How can tha tell me that?"

"That boy what damned you?" he says, spittle goin' everywhere. "He's a liar. He's been caught out. Came back late home one day and makes up a story, cuz he's heard all them things about them Pendle witches, so his father don't beat him! His dad, Mr. Robinson, he's took money off them what he'd not get his boy to accuse of witchcraft. Them what don't pay, little Edmund's been tellin' on for witches!"

I grip the bars so tight, so hopefully, I feel I could prise 'em apart with my bare 'ands. "It's over then!" I say, overjoyed. "I'm goin' to be let go!"

"Aye," he says, "tha'll be acquitted. Tha'll ne'er see daylight again, though."

"Eh? They can't keep me 'ere if they've no cause, if I'm not going to trial. I may not be the brightest, but I know that."

"Nay," he says to me. "Tha knows that tha mun pay for thy board and food 'ere, don't tha? Well, tha's been 'ere so lang nah, reckon tha owes us more than tha could ever see, bein' the kind o' girl tha is."

"Then," I asks, "how shall I ever come by leavin' again?"

And he laughs in me face. "How tha comes and 'ow tha goes is none concern o' mine, lass. All I cares about is keepin' thee away from these locks." And he goes down the passage, laughin' as he goes.

I never paid much mind to the years, except to see their passing with the turning of the seasons before, and now I've lost count of winters I've spent huddlin' in the corner for warmth, or the summer in want of water. The faces of them what come and go with me through this cell, they're like mist. Them wha' I came in 'ere wi', a few got took 'ome again, but the rest… They're all dead now. Just me left. Just me left, again. One girl, she were in 'ere wi' 'er mam and dad, and they both died. Sickness come took 'em. I tried to look after her a bit, but then, she showed the signs o' jail fever, just like they 'ad. At the end, when it were bad, she said that she could see her mam and dad, waitin' for her just beyond the bars. I asked her who else she could see:

"Can tha see a lad, littler than 'e should be, looks daft? Can tha see a girl, pretty, but what's laughin' and cryin' at the same time? Can tha see a woman, wi' eye what don't match, one up here and another down here? SHe's probably lookin' reight angry, at me? Can tha see an old woman, really old, what can't see reight well? Can tha see 'em? Are they there?" But she never answered me. Nor nothin' no more.

Do you know, I've 'ad time to think plenty since I were brought 'ere and it's become my reckonin' - and it is just mine - but I reckon there aren't such things as witches. Not in the way that people think there's witches. If me mam, and Granny, and none o' them what I knew weren't, then I don't think I've known one. I reckon witches are easy to blame. It's simpler and takes less from thee to say 'A witch must 'a' hexed me', than to realise maybe God doesn't favour thee. That maybe bad things just happen sometimes. Don't mean it's a witch. If all that were needed for one to be a witch, was to do as much bad as they could to whoever they could do it to, even them what never crossed 'em, then to me, Roger Nowell was the best - and the worst - witch I've ever known.

Yet I also think, that if there truly were a witch among us, just one out of all of us, I reckon it'd 'ave to be me. I said words... And with those words, I made people die. I might have even made mesen die, all them years ago, and never even knew it.

They'd probably cut me tongue out for what I've told you. About Mr. Nowell, and them what's in power. They try and make you blame the witches, and if there's no witches to blame, they find some. Don't be fooled. They can 'ave my tongue for the good it'll do 'em. And do you know what? I don't care no more.

Nobody will make me say nothin' again.

Final Note By The Author

<u>Folkestone, 8th of February, 2018</u>

Reading back over what I've created here, I realise there seems to be a theme developing out of my writing at this stage(!) Not a difficult-to-find one either. It seems I'm addicted to tragedy, yet simultaneously, I'm unapologetic about that. One of the most powerful things, in my opinion, one can do is make one's audience feel sympathy for people whom they've never met. Society may try at times to make us feel as if it is only natural to identify with a particular closed tribe, and shun all others who are not of our race, background, class, or [insert arbitrary and unimportant defining factor here]. And yet realising that is not what community is about, not what human nature is really about, is what helps understand how human beings have coexisted and helped one another and therefore survived this far.

At the end of the day, the work written here are just plays. Intended to entertain and draw on possibilities as opposed to presenting unbridled fact. I've used artistic licence and allowed inspiration to take me where stories can go. While I've painted here three women who may engender a lot of loyalty and sympathy, we've no way of knowing all the circumstances of any of their lives, and it would be almost impossible to create a completely factual account in this medium. For example: while Oscar treated her shockingly, even in a play where she is the heroine, it's preposterous to show Constance as lily-white in conscience. She was not: she could be judgemental, naive, her apparent favouritism of one son over the other is unsettling, and one could argue she was not strong enough to be the woman who could have come out of such a turn of events on top. Similarly, with the story of Jennet, while one may feel she has been terribly hard done by at the end of her life, my story is only one possibility of many, and despite including many factual aspects, could be completely wrong. She may have been a vindictive and truly wicked little child and led a similarly bitter and angry adulthood, refusing to accept guilt for a calamitous event that she essentially made possible. The fact is, we don't know. But stories and possibilities such as this, in a time where it's all too easy to separate ourselves from our fellow human beings, should be explored.

At the time of writing, I am still touring these shows. To keep up with any performances I'm bringing to your area, please follow the link to :

www.sladewolfe.com/shows

I hope to bring out a second volume of some kind - though it would be nice to have some happier stories to tell as well - at some point in the future. Thank you for your support in buying this book, and I hope, if nothing else, it gives you some spark of inspiration. When I stepped onstage to do my first one woman show, *The Witch In The Woods* – a show that I had written no less – I was terrified, and thought it would be a one-off occurrence, probably too traumatic for my introverted and imposter-syndrome-riddled nature. Now, I run shows back to back, being nervous before a show is an exception, and I absolutely love what I do. If I myself, of all people, can overcome that crippling self-doubt and many years of imposter syndrome to tell these stories - to find these stories, and be found by them - then what can you do?

The wonderful answer is - anything. And don't let anyone, not even yourself, tell you otherwise.

Thanks again, and I hope you've enjoyed the book.

Select Bibliography

Mrs. Oscar Wilde

1. Constance Lloyd to Otho Lloyd, 3rd Sept 1878. MSS Collection of Merlin Holland.
2. Constance Lloyd to Otho Lloyd, Letter Undated. MSS Collection of Merlin Holland.
3. Constance Lloyd to Otho Lloyd, Letter Undated (c. Sept 1878). MSS Collection of Merlin Holland.
4. Constance Lloyd to Otho Lloyd, 25 July 1878. MSS Collection of Merlin Holland.
5. Constance Lloyd to Otho Lloyd, 21 Sept 1878. MSS Collection of Merlin Holland.
6. Ibid.
7. Constance Lloyd to Otho Lloyd, 1 Aug 1880. MSS Collection of Merlin Holland.
8. Constance Lloyd to Otho Lloyd, Letter Undated (1880). MSS Collection of Merlin Holland.
9. Ibid.
10. Constance Lloyd to Otho Lloyd, 10 June 1881. MSS Collection of Merlin Holland.
11. Constance Lloyd to Otho Lloyd, 4 Sept 1880. MSS Collection of Merlin Holland.
12. Constance Lloyd to Otho Lloyd, 10 June 1881. MSS Collection of Merlin Holland.
13. Constance Lloyd to Otho Lloyd, 7 June 1881. MSS Collection of Merlin Holland.
14. Constance Lloyd to Otho Lloyd, 10 June 1881. MSS Collection of Merlin Holland.
15. Constance Lloyd to Otho Lloyd, 23 and 24 Nov 1883. MSS Collection of Merlin Holland.
16. Constance Lloyd to Otho Lloyd, 20 Aug 1882. MSS Collection of Merlin Holland.
17. Ibid.
18. Ibid.
19. Constance Lloyd to Oscar Wilde, addressed from 1 Ely Place, dated Thursday 8.30pm (Thurs 27 Nov 1883) British Library, Eccles Collection, MS 81690.
20. Constance Lloyd to Otho Lloyd, 4 Sept 1880. MSS Collection of Merlin

21. Constance Lloyd to Otho Lloyd, 26 Nov 1883. MSS Collection of Merlin Holland.
22. Constance Lloyd to the Harrises, March 1884.
23. Constance Lloyd to Otho Lloyd, 26 Nov 1883. MSS Collection of Merlin Holland.
24. Joy Melville, *Mother of Oscar: The Life of Jane Francesca Wilde* (John Murray, London, 1994), p.179
25. Otho Lloyd to Nellie Hutchison, Date Unknown. Quoted in: Franny Moyle, *Constance: The Tragic And Scandalous Life of Mrs. Oscar Wilde* (John Murray, London, 2011), p.69
26. Constance Lloyd to Otho Lloyd, 27 Nov 1883. MSS Collection of Merlin Holland.
27. Constance Lloyd to Otho Lloyd, 26 Nov 1883. MSS Collection of Merlin Holland.
28. Constance Wilde to Otho Lloyd, 3 June 1884. MSS Collection of Merlin Holland.
29. Ibid.
30. Ada Leverson, *Letters to the Sphinx from Oscar Wilde: With Reminiscences of the Author* (Duckworth, London 1930), p.44
31. Oscar Wilde to Constance Wilde, , 16 Dec 1884. MSS Collection of Merlin Holland.
32. Constance Wilde to Otho Lloyd, 25 June 1884. MSS Collection of Merlin Holland.
33. Constance Wilde to Lady Mount-Temple 8 Dec 1892. University of Southampton, Broadlands Archive 57/14/6.
34. Constance Wilde to Otho Lloyd, March 1888. MSS Collection of Merlin Holland.
35. Ibid.
36. Merlin Holland and Rupert Hart-Davis, *The Complete Letters of Oscar Wilde* (Fourth Estate, London, 2000) p. 297.
37. Constance Wilde to Lady Mount-Temple 23 Jan 1891. University of Southampton, Broadlands Archive 44/2.
38. Constance Wilde to Lady Mount-Temple 27 Nov 1890. University of Southampton, Broadlands Archive 57/11/3.
39. Constance Wilde to Lady Mount-Temple 20 Nov 1891. University of Southampton, Broadlands Archive 57/12/16.
40. Constance Wilde to Otho Lloyd, March 1888. MSS Collection of Merlin Holland.
41. Constance Wilde to Lady Mount-Temple 20 Nov 1891. University of Southampton, Broadlands Archive 57/12/16.
42. Constance Wilde to Lady Mount-Temple, undated. University of Southampton, Broadlands Archive 57/14/93.
43. Merlin Holland and Rupert Hart-Davis, *The Complete Letters of Oscar Wilde* (Fourth Estate, London, 2000) p. 633. Undated, c.28 Feb 1895
44. Constance Lloyd to Unknown Recipient, April 1896.
45. Lord Alfred Bruce Douglas, *Oscar Wilde: A Summing Up*, (1940), p.99.

46. Constance Holland to Otho Lloyd, 19 Feb 1898. MSS Collection of Merlin Holland.

ABOUT THE AUTHOR

Lexi spent her childhood between her hometown of Sheffield, and Multan in Pakistan. She set her designs on being an actress at age eleven. After finishing her Masters Degree in Acting from LIPA, she moved to London and debuted her first one woman show in November of 2014. She shot her award-winning first short film, *Learning To Talk*, around the same time.

At the time of writing, Lexi lives in Folkestone with her best friend Andrew, with whom she runs Slade Wolfe Enterprises Ltd. Lexi and Andrew tour their shows about the U.K. and are currently working towards several screen productions.

They are considering adding a dog to the family.

www.lexiwolfe.com
www.imdb.me/lexiwolfe
www.sladewolfe.com
www.facebook.com/LexiWolfeOfficialPage
www.twitter.com/lexiwolfe
www.instagram.com/lexiwolfeactress

Printed in Great Britain
by Amazon